Praise for Shelley Bradley's *A Perfect Match*

Rating: 5 Blue Ribbons! "Shelley Bradley is one of my favorite authors for a reason. Her talent is limitless and releases like A PERFECT MATCH further my admiration of this brilliant author."

~ *Romance Junkies*

Rating: 5 Clovers! "A PERFECT MATCH is a wonderfully realistic romance that packs plenty of heat and lots of heart!"

~ *Ck2s Kwips & Kritiques*

"This author knows how to take a happy ending and make you feel it clear down to your toes. A Perfect Match sizzles with energy and passion. Very highly recommended."

~ *Two Lips Reviews*

Joyfully Recommended! "A Perfect Match is pure delight from beginning to end. If you like your books sizzling, fast-paced, with some truly sigh-worthy romantic moments, then Ms. Bradley's newest tale is your perfect match."

~ *Joyfully Reviewed*

"You'll want to devour this captivating and pleasurable...then re-read it again and again."

~ RRTErotic

Look for these titles by

Shelley Bradley

Now Available:

Sneak Peek: Watch Me
The Lady and the Dragon
Naughty Little Secret

A Perfect Match

Shelley Bradley

A Samhain Publishing, Ltd. publication.

Samhain Publishing, Ltd.
577 Mulberry Street, Suite 1520
Macon, GA 31201
www.samhainpublishing.com

A Perfect Match

Print ISBN: 978-1-60504-143-8
Digital ISBN: 978-1-60504-012-7

Editing by Angela James
Cover by Scott Carpenter

First Samhain Publishing, Ltd. electronic publication: May 2008
First Samhain Publishing, Ltd. print publication: March 2009

Chapter One

"Next," John Cannon yelled from the open doorway of his corner office.

"Next victim, he means," Mitch MacKinnon muttered, rising from his desk. "That's me."

"Give me a break." His co-worker Dave rolled his eyes as he sat at his desk behind Mitch's. "You're his star sports writer. He probably saved you the best of Sandra's scoops."

"Like what? The gossip column?"

"No, I got that, along with wedding and birth announcements." He tore off his glasses and rubbed the bridge of his nose. "Oh, I wish that woman hadn't gone into labor early."

Mitch laughed and clapped his co-worker on the back. "I'll ask her to consult you next time."

"Happy Thanksgiving to you, too," Dave called after him. "Asshole."

Picking his way through the maze of computer- and paper-laden desks with a laugh, Mitch strode to his boss's office. Why had John chosen to give him his temporary assignments last? Probably because his editor knew he wouldn't like them.

Mitch rapped on John's open door. "You wanted to see me?"

John looked up from the mountain of paperwork and call-back slips littering his desk. “Stop looking at me like I’m going to rain out the Super Bowl, and close the door.”

Mitch shut the door, then slouched into the room’s lone chair, across from John’s desk. “So what did you save for me? Obituaries?”

“Something better.”

John was upbeat as often as the Vatican elected a new Pope. Mitch raised a skeptical brow. “You’re giving me ‘Community Happenings’, aren’t you?”

“You make it sound as terrible as art reviews.”

“It doesn’t exactly rival the NFL playoffs.”

“But it’s perfect for you. It could use your sense of humor in Sandra’s absence.”

Mitch shrugged. “Try Dave. He’s a funny guy.”

“He’s also married, and what I have in mind requires a single man’s perspective.”

“That’s reverse discrimination.”

“That’s life.”

But “Community Happenings”? Talk about paying your dues.

Mitch gritted his teeth. “You have a particular story in mind for me to start with?”

John crossed the dingy gray floor and pulled open the top drawer of his filing cabinet. He withdrew a brochure and tossed it across his desk. “Ever heard of these people?”

Mitch picked up the slick sepia-tinted flyer, depicting attractive singles on one side. On the other, couples held hands and embraced, their expressions so sweet, they gave him a cavity. At the top, three words that made him groan: *A Perfect Match.*

"Yeah, they got my address six months ago. Hardly a week goes by that they don't remind me I could be meeting my ideal mate." He managed not to choke. Barely.

"Check them out. Write a couple of articles. Visit past and present clients. Interview the owner. Her name is Juliette Lowell. She's an interesting woman, at least according to my wife. They have the same hairdresser."

Mitch frowned, trying to catch John's gaze. His boss wouldn't look him in the face. No doubt about it, something was deeply wrong with this story and Ms. Lowell, judging from John's behavior and the fact Louise Cannon had a hand in it. In fact, the whole thing stunk worse than a landfill.

He stared at his boss in suspicion. "You're up to something. Spill it."

"What makes you say that?"

"Give it a rest. I've worked here for over a year. I know when you're cooking up a scheme."

John shrugged, the picture of a kindly, fifty-something bystander. "I'm not cooking up any scheme, just giving you one of Sandra's assignments."

Yeah, and he'd win a Pulitzer Prize tomorrow writing about the next local softball tournament. Knowing John wasn't going to confess, Mitch chose another tactic. "Don't you have something...meatier. I mean, a dating service? Come on. How about *real* news?"

John shook his head. "Not Sandra's assignment. We pull most of that off of the AP. Besides, we don't have the money to ship your ass to wherever to chase stories. And I think you'll find you have a knack for this."

"*What*? A knack for writing fluff?" Downright insulted, Mitch stood to leave.

"Sit down!" John paused and sighed. "All right. You and I both know you're too talented to be stuck at *The Signal* for long. I'm trying to help you."

"By having me cover 'Community Happenings'?"

"Believe it or not, yes."

Mitch watched in silence as John rose and paced the five steps across his tiled office. "Russ Kendrick is a buddy of mine. We started together twenty years ago at the *L.A. Times*."

Mitch sat again. "Russ Kendrick, as in the editor-in-chief of *USA Today*?"

John smiled. "The same. If you do me this favor, I could mention your name to him."

Mitch leaned across John's desk. Damn, the chance of a lifetime, and he was playing a game of semantics. "You could or you will?"

"God, you have nerve." John laughed. "I *will* mention your name to him, but not until you can prove your versatility. He likes flexible team players. This story might impress him with your range."

"I appreciate what you're trying to do, but how will this fluff prove much of anything to one of the most influential journalists in the country?"

"He likes his staff writers to have the ability to stretch. A long way. This ought to be a good start."

Stretch? Hell, this would make him a contortionist.

John assumed a putting stance in the middle of his minuscule office and practiced his follow-through. "Your first installment is due next Monday."

Mitch stilled the ripe curse hovering on his tongue. John had boxed him into a nice, neat corner using his own ambition. Granted, accepting the assignment was a gamble...but one he might have to take if he wanted to get out of suburban paper hell. After all, John's small mention to Russ Kendrick was more than he would have gotten otherwise.

Mitch sighed. "You have a particular slant in mind?"

John shook his head. "Nope. Go with what feels right to you."

Mitch paused. A dating service? Nothing would ever feel right about this type of story. What kind of people paid good money for this crap? Only the desperate. And what kind of woman started such a business? She had to be a scam artist. After all, when did a bunch of stupid questions and five minutes of videotape ever predict interpersonal chemistry?

"Any questions?" John asked, doing his best impression of Tiger Woods's swing, despite his sagging belly.

Mitch shook his head and rose. "No, I'll go out now and start acting like a 'versatile team player'."

And hope Russ Kendrick doesn't laugh me out of journalism.

☙

Mitch glanced at his watch. 9:10. He'd made an appointment with Ms. Lowell's receptionist to meet at 9:30. So he was a little early. Big deal. He wanted this article researched and written ASAP. The sooner he finished with "Community Happenings", the sooner he could return to *real* writing, even if it was just sports. For now. The sooner John would mention him to Russ Kendrick.

He jumped out of his truck, locking it behind him with a beep. A Perfect Match was nestled in a newer part of Santa Clarita, which had cropped up during the last decade. The office sat in a strip mall, situated between an uptown day spa and a restaurant that billed itself as The Brunchery, whatever that was.

Welcome to a new world of romance and relationships, the window's poster read, above people making middle-school goo-goo eyes at one another. He groaned. Since John insisted on assigning him fluff, why couldn't the man have given him something simple, like the upcoming holiday bazaar?

The late November wind sliced through the morning air. Mitch lifted the collar of his leather jacket around his ears and dashed into A Perfect Match. The receptionist's chair sat empty.

"Hello? Anyone here?"

No reply. *Odd.* But maybe in a good way. If no one was here, maybe he could sneak around a bit, get a little scoop, see if he could find out what kind of business Juliette Lowell ran.

Mitch ventured past the reception area and took about a dozen steps down the hallway. He peeked into the first opening on his left. Nothing but a photocopier, a fax machine and a half-empty coffee pot.

Had everyone left? Maybe they'd gone to The Brunchery.

Scowling, he wandered farther down the hall, past a series of framed wedding pictures, presumably of various clients. He peered at Sarah and Lucas, June 17, 2006. They looked pretty normal. So did Jessica and Matthew, married March 3, 2007. He shrugged. Looks could be deceiving.

A streak of light beaming through a three-inch crack in the last door caught his attention. Ms. Lowell's office? He prowled another few steps to the open door at the end of the hall. Leaning against the frame, he peered inside.

His first sight was of a blonde on all fours with a truly beautiful ass in the air. Her shapely rear end, sheathed in a pencil-slim red skirt, outlined the alluring curve of her waist and hips. Spectacular. Man, what he wouldn't love to do to a naked woman with her curves in that tempting position...

Lengths of golden hair hung over her shoulders, flowing almost to her hands. From the posterior view anyway, she was definitely worth looking at.

"Ugh! This is the second time in a week," she muttered, combing the carpet beside her desk, clearly searching for something. "Thank God it's Friday."

Out of the corner of his eye, Mitch noticed a flicker of something less than a foot from her knee. Hunching down, he retrieved the item. The back to an earring. Its loss could be devastating, according to his sister. Maybe rescuing this damsel from her distress would score him some points.

"Is this what you're looking for?" he asked, holding the little gold back in his palm.

With a startled shriek, she whipped her gaze toward him, hand plastered to her chest.

"Sorry. I didn't mean to scare you." He thrust the earring back closer to her, his eyes glued to her face.

For a moment, Mitch couldn't breathe. The mass of golden hair she'd swept away from her face with a clip accentuated the classical beauty of her high cheekbones and the full lips she'd tinted a sheer, sexy red.

She glanced at the object in his palm, then reached for the small gold item. Her short nails at the tips of her long fingers were painted red, too. "Thank you."

For a brief moment, Mitch thought about dressing her in red. Lace—and nothing else.

"I—I didn't hear you come in."

Everything about her made his lust flame red.

He grinned. "I kind of got that impression, Miss..."

"Juliette Lowell." She refastened her earring with the back

he'd returned to her, then rose to her seemingly average height, and held out her hand.

With shock waves running through his body, he shook it. This was Juliette Lowell, the scam artist? He barely held in a wolf whistle. She was the most gorgeous con he'd ever seen, with blue-green eyes and honey-colored skin. If she was Louise Cannon's idea of interesting, he'd call his boss's wife Loose Cannon a little less often.

"I don't usually greet people on the floor." She blushed sweetly, wearing a wry smile.

Perky yet vulnerable; she made it an interesting combination. Since he'd gotten a mouth-watering view of her backside, he couldn't help stealing a discreet glance at her front. Oh, hell. The drool-worthy sights continued. Her luscious breasts were covered by a sheer white blouse.

He swallowed. "I don't usually sneak up on people in their office."

"My receptionist is out sick. Do you have an appointment?"

"Sort of, but I'm a little early." Mitch withdrew a business card from his shirt pocket. "I'm Mitch MacKinnon, from *The Santa Clarita Signal.*"

Oh, hell. It was *him. Showtime...*

Juliette took his card and glanced at it. *Mitchell E. MacKinnon.* A gorgeous stranger who, right now anyway, had a whole lot of power over her business.

With a nod, she sat behind her desk. *Professional,* she reminded herself. *No gawking at those mile-wide shoulders.*

"I'm glad you could make it. Have a seat. Coffee?"

"No, thanks. I try to avoid the stuff."

"You're a brave soul." She took another sip from her cup.

"I'm really excited by this interview. So, what would you like to know?"

He lowered himself into the chair directly across and took out a small scratch pad and a pencil from his pocket. "Let's start with the basics. How long have you been in business?"

Juliette tried to pay attention to Mitch's question. But her mind wandered off. Lord, he was good-looking. She'd been expecting an Ed Asner-type, salty, older. Instead, she got a hunk who bulged in all the right places under his black T-shirt, with dark, disheveled hair, and a pair of killer dimples. And his jeans clung nicely, faded in places she shouldn't be contemplating since she'd only met the guy two minutes ago.

"Ms. Lowell?" he prompted. "Do you need me to repeat the question?"

He'd caught her staring. Oh, how humiliating. Why didn't she just jump in his lap? "I've been in business officially for three years. I started because I discovered in college that I had a knack for matchmaking."

He scribbled a few notes. "Where did you go to school?"

The black spikes of his lashes surrounded piercing dark eyes. Heaven help her; he even had sleek eyebrows. "Cal Berkeley. I majored in psychology."

"So why did you get away from psychology to become a professional matchmaker?"

The same question her father had asked. "As I said, I discovered I had a talent for knowing when people belonged together." She folded her shaking hands together. "After school, I just decided to combine my education and my ability."

He jotted a few more notes. "Are you using the same method you did at Berkeley?"

Concentrate. Focus on his questions, not staring into his

stunning, suck-you-in, chocolate eyes.

She cleared her throat. "For the most part, yes. Of course, I'm on a much larger scale now. And my process is a little more formal than it used to be, but I still get to know to all my clients individually."

"How many do you have?"

She smiled, trying to appear calm. Not an easy feat with labored breathing. "As of last Friday, I have one thousand, one hundred two. That's down two from the week before. They got married."

He noted that. "In your promotional materials and on your Web site, you advertise your service as one-of-a-kind. Why?"

"Personal attention. The other is method. I combine my gut instinct with a personality inventory, an astrological chart and—"

"Astrology?" he interrupted in disbelief.

"It's more helpful than you might think."

"It's incredibly unscientific."

"So is dating, Mr. MacKinnon."

"But there must be something more...organized, more proven."

She cleared her throat. "I understand your misgivings. Some of my clients had the same doubts at first. The truth is, every good matchmaker has her own method and a good intuition."

He thrust his pad onto the corner of her desk. "But these people are desperate, and you're offering them astrology and intuition."

"Often, that's just what they want, since their own instincts are unsuccessful. I also give them a handwriting analysis. After the personal interview, I add a few observations of my own, input the information into the computer program I had specially written, and out pops a list of possibilities."

His grunt mocked her. "What kind of success rate can that hodgepodge possibly produce?"

Wonderful. Her gorgeous reporter, the one who could really send her business soaring, was a huge disbeliever. Just her luck. "Currently, it's sixty-two percent."

He picked up his pad and wrote again. "Since you use such...unusual methods, don't you worry about lawsuits?"

Gritting her teeth, Juliette inhaled a deep breath. Just like her father, Mitch was a doubter in anything he couldn't see, hear, taste, smell or touch. If it wasn't tangible, it didn't exist. "The vast majority of my clients are quite satisfied."

"But for those who aren't?"

He was cocky, so sure her service was hoopla. Well, if he wanted tangible, she would give it to him. "No one has attempted to sue me to date. In fact, I'd be happy to arrange a time for you to meet with my newest newlyweds. Their happiness will speak for A Perfect Match better than I can."

End of interview, at least as far as she was concerned. What more could she say at the moment that would convince him? Nothing. Words weren't nearly as concrete as newlyweds.

Juliette rose and paused by his chair, arms crossed. Mitch only settled against the back of his chair with his lips curled up, as if suppressing a smile of victory.

"You're not very anxious to talk to me, Ms. Lowell."

"On the contrary, I'm eager to talk to a reporter, but not one who has prejudged my concept before the interview is finished."

His deprecating laugh was almost as irritating as dismissive attitude. "You have to admit your methods seem a little bizarre."

"Only to your type," she shot back.

His raised brows told Juliette she had his full attention again. "And what type is that?"

"Oh—" she tossed a casual hand through the air, "—an extravert with a strong sensing tendency. You're obviously a thinking type without a lot of boundaries. I'd guess you're an ESTP."

"Huh?"

"And that aura you give off, that air of cockiness... Are you a Scorpio by chance?"

Mitch's frown hovered between confusion and disbelief. "Yeah."

She nodded, a smile hovering on her lips. "You're not from California, are you?"

He paused. "No. Indiana."

"That partially explains your rejection of all but the tried and true. The rest is in personality and upbringing." She sat on the edge of the desk, enjoying the dramatic effect of her pause. Mitch hung on her every movement. "You're primarily a sports writer, I heard. I'll bet you were a jock with aspirations."

He scowled. "I'm interviewing you. Can we get back to it?"

"Touchy subject, is it?"

He scanned his notes. "Are *you* married?"

She paused. "Not at the moment."

His head popped up, gaze challenging. "If you're so good at predicting chemistry between men and women, why doesn't Juliette have a Romeo?"

She held her tongue. She didn't owe Mr. Concrete an explanation about Andrew, her seemingly ideal mate, and why she hadn't yet responded to his proposal. How could she tell Mitch what she couldn't even explain to herself?

"Your article is about my business. Do you have anything else along that line you'd like to cover?"

He smiled faintly. "Not right now, but I'd like to meet your newlyweds."

"Fine. I'll arrange a meeting for tomorrow, if possible." Juliette drifted toward her office door.

Mitch followed suit. "Just give me a call."

When he reached for her hand, Juliette took it with reluctance. Nothing in their handshake was unbusinesslike, yet that same head-to-toe tingle that plagued her on their first such contact swarmed her again.

As he backtracked down the hall, she followed. His dark hair touched the bottom of his collar with a slight curl. The span of his wide shoulders, encased in black leather, filled her vision. She had no doubt he worked out diligently and often. Her eyes gravitated to the worn seat of his jeans clinging to his well-formed behind.

She was leering like a teenager. What was the matter with her?

Nothing. There was nothing wrong with simple attraction between a healthy man and woman. It happened every day, to thousands of people. This feeling didn't mean there was anything wrong with her relationship with Andrew.

But why Mitch MacKinnon? He was a cocky jerk with hang-ups about anything not tangible. She'd bet he had never even meditated.

"Thank you for your time." The line sounded as phony as "What's your sign?"

"My pleasure," she said, trying to maintain a smile.

Mitch MacKinnon was a know-it-all. Definitely not for her. So why was her matchmaking intuition on alert? She had this tingling certainty often—around clients. But she'd never experienced this sensation in a relationship of her own. What did that mean?

Maybe nothing. Did it *have* to mean something? Maybe it was the stormy weather, a full moon or just too many hormones.

She knew one way to cinch it. "Mr. MacKinnon, do you believe in love and commitment? In putting down roots and raising a family?"

At the door, he turned. His gaze travelled a leisurely path down her body. Juliette felt the burn of his gaze all over. Oh, he was thorough...and apparently interested in her, too. Why did that fact make her heart pound? Awareness of him, his obvious maleness evident in his seemingly-casual stance, his body language and scent, assailed her—things she never noticed about Andrew. She swallowed a knot of tension.

"I've never been in love myself." He shrugged. "It makes me wonder if love is just something people talk themselves into because they don't want to be alone. As for putting down roots... I'd rather see the world."

Juliette released her breath. She and Mitch MacKinnon hardly belonged on the same planet, much less the same relationship. Proving that ought to make her happy, right? Of course.

She had Andrew's proposal to concentrate on. She had to decide, had to figure out why she just couldn't say yes to the man who had so sweetly professed his love and offered her the hometown dreams of her childhood.

She cleared her throat. "Feel free to call me if you have any questions after you've interviewed the Grahams."

"Who? Oh, the newlyweds." He nodded, studying her one last time, his dark eyes lingering. "I'll be in touch."

Late that afternoon, Juliette looked up from the fax machine to find her younger sister trudging through the office's front door. Kara dropped her purse and briefcase in the middle of the hall, then pushed her auburn hair from her face with a sigh.

"Ugh! What a terrible day. The job description of a legal secretary should be slave."

Juliette laughed. "They do pay you for your labor."

Her sister snorted. "Enough to see a movie once a month."

"Things will start looking up once we scrape together the money for your tuition to law school. You'll see."

Kara grabbed a Styrofoam cup of coffee and plopped down into a chair. "Did Dad call here for me?"

Juliette paused. "No. He didn't...call your office?"

Kara shook her head and sunk her teeth into her top lip. "Did you check the mail today at lunch?"

Juliette touched a comforting hand on her sister's shoulder. "I'm sorry. I didn't see anything for you."

Kara's face turned red as she fought tears. Her struggle revived Juliette's own resentment. "The bastard forgot my birthday. Again."

Juliette knelt in front of her sister. "If it's any consolation, he never remembers mine, either. That was Mom's job, and when she died..."

The unspoken hung between them. Neither had to mention the long weeks without parental guidance or love. Nothing needed to be said about the numerous cities the Air Force dictated they live in. Juliette had experienced that hurt herself, knew how deep it ran. All she could try to do was cheer Kara up.

"Someday, you'll find a great guy who will remember every occasion, right down to anniversaries each month."

"No, I won't. You know I never fall for sensitive guys like Andrew."

"A ton of good-looking, less-than-sensitive guys are just waiting to meet you, any one of which may be Mr. Right."

Kara sent her a non-committal grunt.

"Did you make any plans tonight?"

"Yeah, I have a date with a gallon of rocky road, which I'll pay for tomorrow with two hours of kick-boxing."

Juliette pulled her sister to her feet. "Let's play Cinderella, instead, like when we were kids. I'll be your Fairy Godmother."

Kara peered at her suspiciously. "What wacky idea do you have now?"

"I was asking you to the ball," Juliette scolded. "Or in this case, the hospital charity dance. Andrew has an extra ticket. Of course, I won't make your dress, but you can borrow something out of my closet."

Kara's face lit up...then fell. "No, you and Andrew go without me. I don't want to be in the way."

Juliette frowned. "Don't be silly. Andrew doesn't mind having you around."

"He does. You just don't want to be alone with him. Why is that?"

She shot her sister a warning glance. "That's not true. We enjoy your company. Are you coming or not?" When Kara still resisted, Juliette pressed on. "Come on. We'll go out for a sinful dessert after our rubber chicken dinner."

Kara cast her a baleful glare and gathered her belongings. "Gosh, you can talk me into anything. It's pathetic."

"I'm your big sister. I know best." She followed Kara down the hall, to the door. "I'll be home in a little while. Andrew will pick us up at seven."

"Thanks. I wasn't looking forward to being alone tonight." Kara reached for the door knob, then turned back. "Oh, I meant to ask you how it went with that reporter this morning?"

Juliette wondered how she could explain that she'd found Mitchell MacKinnon both totally infuriating and incredibly sexy. Andrew fit her description of the perfect husband, but Mitch was the kind of man a girl wanted to get horizontal with for a lost weekend so she could come home sore, hoarse and smiling. She'd always focused more on the long term, the big prize. But since meeting Mr. Sex-on-Two-Legs, Andrew and his proposal had taken a backseat in her thoughts.

Get a grip! Andrew was kind, compassionate, loving, humorous, intelligent. Only a fool wouldn't love him.

Besides, she had a feeling that, no matter what she said, Mitch would use his pen to poison the community against her business, unless the Grahams won him over in a big way. How could she want such a skeptic?

Juliette shrugged in answer to Kara's question. "We'll just have to see what happens."

Chapter Two

Juliette stepped into the hotel's ballroom that evening, dreading the next few hours. Kara, all dolled up in an emerald velvet cocktail dress and a smile, strolled beside her.

How could Kara be excited about this? These events were by no means unusual. And come ten o'clock, the band would be well into their Sing-and-Sway-with-Sammy-Kaye repertoire. She sighed. What she wouldn't give to be home with a pizza and a good book. She knew Andrew had to make an appearance because he was a community leader and Rotary Club member with political hopes. Still, once in a while she wished he'd decline an invitation.

"Did I tell you how gorgeous you look tonight?" Andrew whispered in her ear as he seated her at their table.

Juliette smiled. "At least twice, but thank you."

Andrew sat beside her and took her hand. He frowned when he found it bare. "You'd look even better with your engagement ring. When are you going to give me an answer?"

Juliette withdrew her hand. She had been dreading this question all evening, in fact, all week. "When I've made up my mind."

"I asked you nearly two weeks ago," he pointed out in a low voice. "On Monday, I leave for nearly a month in Milwaukee with that new client. I would love to have your answer before I go."

"I know. And I'm trying, but your proposal really took me by surprise. We've only been dating for two months. I think a decision this important shouldn't be rushed."

Andrew took her hand again, leaning closer. "Darling, what more do you I need? We're good together, and I love you—"

"I just don't want to rush things. Let's be really sure, okay?"

Juliette was spared Andrew's response when some acquaintances took the remaining seats at their table.

"Isn't this exciting?" Kara whispered on her right. "Everyone looks so elegant. I could stare at them for hours."

Juliette sighed and counted the seconds until they could make a discreet exit.

A few minutes later, white-jacketed waiters served dinner. Andrew became engrossed in a conversation with the attorney across the table about voter redistricting and earthquake disaster recovery plans. Kara listened with a rapt ear. Juliette pushed her barely-touched plate aside and excused herself to escape to the rest room.

As she passed a row of tables outlining the dance floor, a familiar voice called out, "Juliette."

Mitch MacKinnon.

She recognized the voice right away by the shiver in her spine. Slowly, she turned. He deserved a Hunk of the Year award for the way he shaped a tuxedo jacket and his drop-dead dimpled smile.

Juliette inhaled, hoping oxygen would revive her suddenly malfunctioning brain. "Hi."

"Hi, yourself." He rose, eyeing the bared shoulders above her rosy gown intently. "Wow. This morning, I didn't think you could look much better. What an idiot I was."

Juliette actually felt heat crawl up her face. "Thank you."

"Hey, since you look so good, and I'm all dressed up in this penguin suit, how about a dance?"

"Aren't you with someone?"

"Yeah, but she's gone to the bathroom."

He was asking her to dance when his date had only slipped out for a moment? Though he wasn't making a play for her exactly, asking her to dance when he was here on a date seemed like a really asshole thing to do. "Don't you think she'll mind?"

"Nah," he assured, grinning. "My mother has accepted the fact I have other women in my life since puberty."

"You're here with your mother?"

He nodded, his smile faltering. "She moved out here when Dad died. Part of the deal was that I'd escort her to these fancy wing-ding parties."

So he wasn't a jerk—at least not totally. "That's...considerate of you."

He shrugged. "So how 'bout it?"

Juliette hesitated. Looking at Mitch was unnerving enough, but touching him and letting him touch her when she was wearing a backless dress... None of that seemed wise.

"I really should get back—"

"Oh, come on. Three minutes," he cajoled, stepping closer. *God, he smells fabulous.* "I'll ask you a few questions. It'll be the second part of our interview."

She met his dark stare with a quiver. "You're difficult to turn down."

"Thanks for not trying too hard."

Juliette felt his fingertips at her elbow a moment later. His exhalations caressed the tingling skin of her neck. When they reached the perimeter of the dance floor, Mitch turned her into his arms.

His expression devoured her.

Juliette swallowed, unable to tear her gaze away. He slid his hand up the length of her arm and around to her bare back. Tingles danced all over her skin, through her body. *Oh, wow!* Reaching for her other hand with his, he swayed to the music.

Having Mitch's strong arms around her felt like an embrace. She responded to it, heard her own breathing roughen in answer to his touch. His scent, teasing, musky, tickled her nose. Every pore opened to bask in his male aura. Every nerve strained toward him.

Deep within, her matchmaking intuition sparked, a gut feeling signaling that Mitch could be special to her.

Impossible. He wasn't even sure love existed and was more interested in seeing the world than raising a family.

Then why did she feel this...deep curiosity to know Mitch, experience his every facet? Why did she want nothing more than to cast their differences aside and know the taste of his kiss?

"Nice music, huh?" He mocked the band's selection.

Until he'd mentioned the blaring trumpets, she hadn't noticed. She sent Mitch a shaky smile. "Fine."

"Listen, about this morning... My turf is sports, and I'm a little cranky about having to cover 'Community Happenings'. I'm sorry."

Juliette met his gaze. Before she could drown in his dark, smoky eyes, she forced herself to reply, "Does your change of heart mean you believe in my methods now?"

He smiled ruefully. “No. It just means I could have been more polite in my disbelief.”

Not what she wanted to hear, but at least he was honest. Still, his write-up would affect her fledgling business. “Aren’t reporters supposed to be objective?”

“Ah, yes. The ‘impartial observer of life’ theory.” He twirled her around. “I’m an opinionated guy. That’s one reason my beat is sports. You’re supposed to tell it like it is.”

“All right. What would it take to change your mind?”

With a shrug, he answered, “It’s just not the kind of stuff I believe in, you know, astrology and handwriting analysis. But I’m willing to meet the Grahams and see your business from their point of view.”

His hand drifted down her bare back in something dangerously close to a caress. He fit her body closer to his, and Juliette almost lost her reply in the feel of his hard body against her own, in the thundering of her heart.

“I’m glad you’re keeping an open mind,” she squeaked out.

Mitch felt steady, substantial, like a thousand-year-old redwood. She allowed her hand to drift up the sleek, solid curve of his shoulder, her fingers pressing into his firm flesh. In his arms, surrounded by his scent, her imagination was beginning to let loose, complete with visions of she and Mitch in front of a roaring fire, naked and—

“Are you from Santa Clarita?” He spoke in a whisper, hushed as if it belonged among the tangled sheets of lovers. She’d never realized how arousing a man’s voice could be.

Juliette understood now, when her nipples stood up and all but begged for attention.

He laid his cheek against hers. His breath fanned into her ear. Shivers raced across her skin. Juliette knew she ought to pull away, and planned to...in a minute.

“No. Have you lived here long?” she asked, her own voice breathy.

Out of the corner of her eye, she spotted Andrew twirling Kara across the sparsely-populated dance floor. The sight of her almost-fiancé jolted Juliette back to reality.

She and Mitch were dancing too close for acquaintances. With faces touching and mouths inches apart...what would Andrew think? A glance across the ballroom worried her. Andrew laughed with Kara as he glided across the floor with her, seeming oblivious.

Okay, maybe the better question would be, why did being in Mitch’s arms feel so good? Why was she so tempted by him? He really wasn’t her type.

“I’ve been in Santa Clarita for ten months,” Mitch replied. “Before that, I lived in Vermont, Manhattan and Washington State. I did a brief stint in Birmingham, England.”

Juliette pulled away. “Did you move that much just to see the world?”

“You make it sound like a fatal disease. Moving is exciting, as long as the job is good. Besides, I wasn’t sorry to leave Vermont or Washington. Too cold and rainy. And let’s face facts, it takes a special kind of person to live in Manhattan. I wasn’t special, I guess.”

“Do you plan on staying here now?” she asked, afraid she already knew his answer.

“Here?” Mitch laughed. “Hell, no. I’ve got an outside shot at a job at *USA Today*. If I get it, I’ll be packing up again.”

“And you’re excited by packing boxes, changing phone numbers, moving to yet someplace else where you know no one?”

"New places and people put adventure in your life."

Stability clearly wasn't the name of his game. Why did she find him so interesting when they clearly had so little in common?

"Don't you ever feel..." she groped for a word, "...ungrounded? Like you don't have any roots, any place to really call home? When you move away, don't you ever wonder what kind of happiness you may have left behind?"

The downward slash of his brows and his blank stare shouted confusion. Perfect. He didn't even understand her question. There was no way he'd be able to give her, or himself, an answer.

"Not really. I mean, there's a lot of great people I want to meet and a bunch of exciting places I'm dying to see. Why hang around, if you don't have to?"

She gaped at him, open-mouthed, for a full ten seconds. "Because life is about security and having your friends and loved ones around you. Having someone to share joys and sorrows with. Knowing you'll be comforted by the warm and familiar as you get older."

He frowned. "You sound like my mom. Don't you ever think about all the places you'll never see trapped in this little town? You ever been to Paris? I have. Lived there for three months right after college. I loved it!"

"That's what vacations are for," she bristled.

He rolled his eyes. "You can't really get to know a city in a week. Life may be about security for you. Me? I want to see and do it all. Growing up in a town so small that watching the grass grow thrilled the locals cured me of 'stability'. I don't want to wake up one day, middle-aged and miserable, and lament about all the things I never did, but always wanted to. That's a waste."

Juliette stiffened in his arms. This conversation was

headed nowhere—fast. Mitch, along with his anti-root attitude, only proved that her matchmaking intuition wasn't one hundred percent right.

And her gut feeling was wrong in this case. Andrew had to be the perfect man for her.

Why wasn't her heart convinced of that fact?

Either way, staying in Mitch's arms, inhaling his to-die-for scent and thinking about tangled sheets was just stupid.

Juliette withdrew herself from Mitch and backed away. "I—uh...need to be going. I see my boyfriend across the room waiting for me."

Then she turned and fled.

☙

According to the message Juliette had left him late Friday afternoon, along with directions, Mitch was supposed to meet the Grahams at their house. She had set the interview up for two p.m. on Saturday. Not exactly the way he wanted to spend the afternoon, but the sooner he finished this piece, the sooner he could get on with real journalism writing and his future.

Retrieving the directions from his appointment book, he hopped into his pick-up truck and steered it toward Interstate 5.

It was almost a shame he wouldn't see Juliette Lowell again. No, not almost; it *was* a shame, even if she was unusual. He couldn't fathom how she had known he was a Scorpio from somewhere other than California. By accent? Intuition? And he wasn't sure he even wanted to know what the heck a sensing tendency was.

Despite that, he found her both gorgeous and intriguing.

Smart, her wacky ways aside. So why professional matchmaking with all these hokey theories? Maybe the Grahams would shed a little light.

As for seeing Juliette again...not smart. Dancing with her had been nothing short of pure pleasure, her sweet breasts and bare shoulders all up against him, her soft, catchy breaths and rosy cheeks driving him insane. She'd been aroused. Lord knew he had been. But he was writing an article about her business. Asking her out was bound to cloud his objectivity. Worse, she was involved with someone. But her ring finger was bare, so unless that changed, she wouldn't be off limits after this story.

He arrived at the Grahams' in ten minutes. They greeted him at the door with wide smiles and hands clasped like teenagers. Both Dan and Tina Graham were in their mid-thirties, and seemingly both attractive and smart enough to have found mates without Juliette's help.

They settled in the living room, which was a mix of dark woods and warm fabrics. He smiled at the obvious blending of male and female and withdrew his notebook from his pocket.

"So," he began, "I hear you got married recently."

Tina Graham nodded, her blue eyes bright. "In a small garden ceremony in Malibu. It was beautiful."

She cast a loving glance at her husband. He responded by squeezing her hand.

"She planned everything that way." Dan leaned toward Mitch. "The wedding was perfect, just like her."

Wow, it was thick in here. Was this Juliette's idea of a perfect match, this sappy mush? If so, no thanks.

"Congratulations. When did you two meet?"

"In March," Dan answered. "I'd just gotten involved with A Perfect Match. The first woman Juliette recommended to me was Tina. I wanted children but couldn't have any. Tina already has a darling four-year-old daughter. We both like to hike and read mysteries."

"It was love at first sight," Tina interjected.

No relationship was that easy, ever. "Didn't you two have personal styles to mesh?" At their puzzled looks, he clarified, "You know, issues? He doesn't put the toilet seat down or she shops too much?"

"No," Dan answered. "It was smooth sailing from day one. I asked her to marry me in June. She accepted, and we both decided to have the wedding over Thanksgiving, when our families would be in town."

Mitch shook his head in disbelief. How was he supposed to judge Juliette's business based on two lovesick adults? "So why a dating service? Why didn't you meet anyone through a mutual friend or...in the grocery store or a bar?"

Tina shuddered. "I hate bars."

Dan caressed Tina's back. "We didn't socialize in the same circles, and I avoid the grocery store whenever possible. Without Juliette, we probably would never have met."

"She set me at ease right away," Tina confided. "I felt certain she would match me up with someone great since all her clients are pre-screened." She sent another longing look to her husband. "I was right."

Jeez, their sentiment was like a flowery greeting card. He almost wondered if Juliette had paid them for this plug.

"So what made you think of a dating service?" he asked instead.

"We're both busy," Dan began. "We didn't want to waste time meeting people with whom we had nothing in common."

"Was finding a spouse your goal at the start?"

"Not for me," Tina said. "I've only been divorced three years. I didn't think I was ready to be married again. I just wanted to date a little, get out some. But Dan proved that a different man makes for a whole different experience."

"What about you, Dan? Were you looking for a wife?"

He nodded. "I was thirty-six and had never been married. I was ready, but not sure how to meet the right woman. So I put it in the hands of professionals. Juliette has an amazing track record."

"Are you embarrassed to admit to acquaintances that you met your spouse through a dating service?"

Tina shrugged. "Not really. They're a part of mainstream society."

"Yeah," Dan seconded. "I was more embarrassed about being thirty-six and single. And I came to the conclusion that it doesn't matter where you find love. When it's right, it's worth whatever risk."

Maybe. He'd never given it much thought. Or maybe these people didn't have any social skills. It wasn't impossible they were oblivious to the fact most couples didn't meet their mates through a bunch of questions and a woman's gut instinct. Unless the lovely Ms. Lowell had bamboozled them so completely, they would have paid any price.

☙

Juliette dashed into the office Tuesday morning and pressed the button on her answering machine.

"Hi. It's Mitch MacKinnon from *The Signal*."

Her heart picked up tempo at the sound of his voice. Had he spent most of the weekend thinking about her, too?

"Um...I met with the Grahams on Saturday. The article will be out in today's edition of the paper. My perspective comes mostly from my observations of Dan and Tina, as well as some of the issues we...discussed." He rattled off his cell phone number. "Call me if you have any questions."

Dial tone followed his message, ominous in the wake of his cryptic words. Funny, but his tone sounded almost apologetic. She frowned. After Friday night and their interaction at the charity dance, she'd hoped he had come to understand. Dan and Tina were one of her brightest success stories, as in love as they were. What else could he possibly see in them?

Shrugging, she strode to The Brunchery with her wallet in hand and bought a paper from the machine. She also splurged on a chocolate croissant from inside the bakery case.

She juggled the three items as she made her way back to her office. Once inside, she spread the paper out and began thumbing through it. Letters to the editor, national news, the kid's section. Finally, "Community Happenings". The byline grabbed her attention.

A Perfect Match different, but by no means perfect.

By Mitchell E. MacKinnon.

Juliette's stomach sunk close to her toes as she read the rest of the article.

Dating is difficult. Most everyone has gone out with a friend of a friend, or been on a blind date. For those with few social contacts and a lonely life, a dating service may seem like a prayer answered.

In the case of A Perfect Match, that may not be entirely true.

"What!" Juliette shrieked, her temper flaring. She gripped the newspaper and read on.

The service's owner, Juliette Lowell, is vivacious, energetic and intelligent. She's a woman clearly devoted to her cause, who believes in her business. But on the other side of her self-assurance are her clients, who pay good money and anticipate they'll meet the mate of their dreams.

Fairly or unfairly, many regard the patrons of a dating service as desperate singles. As such, some feel it's irresponsible to take a hopeful customer's money and base a portion of the outcome on such unproven theories as astrology and handwriting analysis. Ms. Lowell combines these "factors" with a personality inventory along the lines of Myers-Briggs Personality Type Indicator, then mixes all of the above with her personal observations. While Ms. Lowell, who received a Bachelor's in Psychology from UC Berkeley, may be regarded as savvy enough to observe the personal hopes and habits of others, one may wonder what kind of results her unscientific method can possibly produce.

Juliette balled a corner of the paper up in her fist. Irresponsible? Unproven? Unscientific? Should love be proven by a theory in his twisted head? She shook her head, her breath coming fast and hard. Unreal!

Her newest newlyweds, as Ms. Lowell calls them, appear to be very mainstream. They are, admittedly, thrilled with A Perfect Match's performance. But they only met a scant eight months ago. They've been man and wife just over a week. Perhaps this relationship will flourish in the long term. Its stability and health will only be borne out with time, as with all marriages. But this soon into the relationship, it may be mere infatuation. A local marriage and family therapist suggested they will have a period of growth and discovery, not all painless, in the next year.

Even if this couple does not beat the divorce statistics, they state one fact clearly: Without Ms. Lowell's service, they probably wouldn't have met each other. And they are very grateful.

Perhaps, but keep in mind that many might regard A Perfect Match in a different light—something fun, like visiting a fortune teller, but nothing a shrewd consumer should take too seriously.

Juliette crushed the entire page into a tiny paper ball.

That pig! That insensitive oaf! She'd spent her weekend mooning over a man who thought nothing of callously bad-mouthing her business? Never mind that Mitchell E. MacKinnon didn't know she'd been thinking about him. He must have sensed her attraction, and by the way he had held her close during their dance Friday night, he returned the interest. So why had he trashed her to the community?

Oh, he'd probably give her a line about mixing business and pleasure. Bullshit! His bias had everything to do with his closed-minded attitude. Fine. If the infuriating man wanted more tangible proof of her ability beyond the Grahams, she'd dang well give it to him. Then she'd make him eat his words. In print.

Mitch heard Juliette's voice raised in anger long before he expected it. He figured he'd see her pacing the visitor's area about noon or so, demanding an explanation to his article.

Instead, she was threading her way through the rows of desks, past gaping reporters, bearing down on him with an angry gleam in her sea-colored eyes. He glanced at his watch. It was just before 10 a.m.

She reached his desk, chest heaving inside a delicate lace blouse, and tossed a crumpled copy of the "Community Happenings" page at him with a snap of her wrist. "This is demeaning. Given my statistics, I would hardly call my business irresponsible."

He stood slowly, pausing to gaze at her flushed cheeks. Today, she wore a short black skirt in some filmy material modern fashion designers termed chic. For something so in style, the garment certainly did wild things to his pulse.

"Aren't you going to say something?" she demanded.

"Juliette—"

"Ms. Lowell," she corrected, teeth clenched.

"Ms. Lowell, I'm sorry you feel I reported on your business inaccurately. I can only say this is what I honestly believe. I am compelled to report facts to the public—"

"Then report the facts, my good track record, my personal care for my clients. Don't report this from your bias."

He had to give her credit. She hung onto her argument with the tenacity of a bulldog. "I believe the average Joe Citizen in this little city will agree with my assessment."

"That's garbage. You took the easy way out by stating your feelings. You judged the Grahams, and me in particular, harshly, when you have no firsthand knowledge of my business."

Mitch leaned closer, bracing his hands against the desk. "I don't have to. You won't find a qualified scientist anywhere in the world who will tell you that astrology is anything but hocus-pocus."

"Dating itself is unscientific. And if it's that much

malarkey, why do so many people read their horoscope every day? I know people who make life decisions based on what planets are in which house."

"Are these the same people who smoke illegal substances and sell macramé art?"

Juliette threw her hands up in the air. "I can't believe it. You're insulting me again."

"That's not what I intended." He took a deep breath. "Look, maybe we should just agree to disagree. What do you say?"

"Absolutely not! Something like this—" she pointed to the article, "—will taint my business in the eyes of the community for months, maybe even years."

"I'm sorry you feel that way."

"Your apology is hardly going to fix the problem."

He shrugged. "So what do you want? A retraction? Because if you do—"

"I don't want handouts," she interrupted. "I'm willing to earn your respect."

Mitch crossed his arms across his chest, brows raised in disbelief. "How do you propose to do that?"

Juliette smiled. He knew he wasn't going to like her idea. "Learn about my business from experience."

"Excuse me?"

"Get to know my service for yourself," she reiterated.

She couldn't be serious, could she? "Are you suggesting I register as one of your clients?"

"Exactly. That way, you'll be well informed."

"No way. I like my life just fine. I don't want to date any flower child, even if it's just once."

"Flower child? You're—"

“Finished,” he cut in. “This story is over.”

Juliette grabbed the paper from her desk. “You haven’t seen the last of me, Mr. MacKinnon. I’ll haunt your office. I’ll write letters to the editor. And I will change your mind.”

With those words, she whirled away. Mitch watched the sharp sway of her retreat as the skirt clung to her ass and exposed lots of her gorgeous legs.

Dave whistled. “She is hot under the collar—and just plain hot. Wow!”

Mitch shot his co-worker a quelling glare. “That’s part of the problem. It’s a damn shame that my professional opinion has to interfere with my hormones.”

“I can tell by the look on your face that she has all of yours raging.”

“Yep.” Mitch sighed. “She doesn’t lack brains or resolve. But I’m not about to stoop to printing a retraction just so I could date her.” Both he and Russ Kendrick would be appalled if he did, and with good reason. He’d jump off a bridge before sacrificing his ethics.

But letting her set him up with someone... Not in this lifetime. Lord knew what kind of wacko he’d end up spending an evening with. No, thank you. He’d rather endure her anger and the regret that they had never shared anything but a dance.

Late that afternoon, Mitch’s phone rang. He picked up the receiver. “MacKinnon here.”

“Mitch, can I see you in my office for a minute?” John Cannon said on the other end of the line. “You’re not going to believe what’s happened.”

"Sure, John," he replied with a sinking feeling Juliette Lowell was involved.

He rose with all the enthusiasm of a condemned man. Next to him, his co-worker and friend Dave laughed. "The dating service thing?"

"I'm betting on it," he muttered and set off for John's office.

"What's up?" he called from just inside his boss's doorway.

"Sit down, Mitch. You've started a real controversy."

"A Perfect Match, right?" He plopped down into the plastic chair across from John's desk.

John nodded. "I've had phone calls and e-mails all day long. Some readers love you. Others hate your guts. But they all mention the same thing: They want more."

"I don't think Ms. Lowell will want that. She and her outrage already paid me a visit today."

"I know. I'd been sitting here half the day, trying to find possible angles for a follow-up, based on the feedback we've had, when Ms. Lowell called."

Oh, no. Trouble with a capital T. "John, I know what you're going to say, but—"

"You've got to do it. Let her fix you up. It's only one evening, and the paper will pay for it."

Mitch hesitated. How on earth could he gracefully decline this scoop? The whole suggestion was just too bizarre. And the amount of crow he'd have to eat if he suddenly agreed with Juliette's plan... He cringed just thinking about it. On the other hand, he'd get to see Juliette again. Even if she hated him, he couldn't muster anything near loathing for her.

"Besides, the kind of increase we're having in circulation is bound to get Russ Kendrick's attention," John added.

John's reminder about the *USA Today* editor was the

proverbial nail in his coffin. With his future on the line, Mitch knew he didn't have much choice but to write the follow up.

He groaned. He was about to have a date with a buckskin-clad hippie who worried if Venus was in her seventh house. Lord knew, he wouldn't be lucky enough to date some semi-normal woman. And after this fiasco, he'd need a miracle to ever get a date with Juliette.

Chapter Three

Late that afternoon, Mitch swallowed every ounce of his pride and drove to Juliette's office. He wasn't sure which he dreaded more: Going on one of her voodoo dates or accepting her challenge after he'd vowed it would never happen.

In the parking lot, he tore off his shades, finger-combed his hair and took a deep breath. Jeez, the things he was willing to do for his career.

When he stepped into A Perfect Match, a business-like, forty-something receptionist sat in the front office.

"I'm Mitch MacKinnon. I'm here to see Ms. Lowell."

She peered down her longish nose at the appointment book on the desk. "You don't have an appointment. Ms. Lowell is very busy. If you'll—"

"She'll see me."

The graying woman cast him a dubious glance and rose from her desk. "I'll ask. Wait here."

The woman disappeared down the narrow, carpeted hallway. Mitch paced. Damn, this was unfair, to have to suffer through Juliette's bizarre ministrations just to gain inside knowledge of her business. She'd never enrolled herself in her own service, he'd bet.

And maybe she should.

A wide grin spread across his face. Of course! He was going to catch her in her own trap. What a follow-up article this would be! Vindication in print; how sweet.

A few moments later, Juliette emerged, wearing that same filmy white lacy/strappy top he'd noticed earlier. His smile faltered. Yeah, he'd have vindication and a juicy scoop, all right. And with it, would go any chance he'd had of ever touching Juliette. Sometimes life sucked.

"What are you doing here, Mr. MacKinnon? Did you come to dig up more dirt?"

Even as Juliette confronted him, she couldn't stop her eyes from making a sweep down his hunky body. Disgusting. Even after the terrible things Mitch had written about her business, he still looked undeniably yummy. Ugh! And those killer dimples...

She shook her head to clear it. Why did she feel irrational whenever he entered the room?

"No. I came for a date. You offered. I'm accepting."

Juliette couldn't have been more stunned if he'd said he was pregnant. Given his vehemence earlier, this had to be some ploy. "Really? What changed your mind?"

He hesitated, his gaze on her face. "My boss. He insisted your suggestion would make the ideal follow-up."

"What else? I thought I'd need an act of God for you to reconsider your opinion."

"Close. The editor-in-chief of *USA Today*. There's a chance this story might catch his eye."

She shook her head. "So you're not really here to change your mind, just impress your present and future bosses?"

"Look, I know you're hacked at me. If the shoe were on the

other foot, I guess I'd be mad, too. But I've got to be honest; your business just doesn't make much sense to me. Business means making something, a product you can sell, or at least a service based on proven theories."

She exhaled in a huff. "You sensing-thinkers can be so closed minded and foolishly ambitious."

"I prefer to think of it as logical and hard working."

Juliette rolled her eyes. "You and my father."

"Do you still want the chance to change my mind or not?"

Juliette tapped her foot. The odds of erasing his doubts were worse than hitting a million dollar jackpot in Las Vegas. Still, she believed in her business and had converted more than a few skeptics in her time. Maybe Mitch was the ultimate challenge. And maybe setting him up with another woman would help to erase him from her thoughts.

"Of course I want to change your mind."

He smiled, and his dimples made her knees go weak. What a sucker she was.

"Good. I've got a counter-challenge of my own."

"I knew you had to be up to something." She glared at him in suspicion. "What?"

"Have you ever put yourself through your own service?"

"*What?*"

"You know, made yourself 'A Perfect Match'."

"Don't be ridiculous. Dating a client would be unethical. Besides, I'm already involved with someone."

"You admitted yourself, you're not married yet."

"No, but he's asked."

Her words hit him like a sucker punch in the gut. Engaged? His jaw tightened. "Your boyfriend will have to understand. This is business. If you want to change my mind, you too have to test the merit of your own service."

"And what do you think your idea will prove?"

Mitch smiled smugly. "Well, when you wind up on a date with someone you can't stand, you'll be forced to admit that my byline read correctly: A Perfect Match is by no means perfect."

"Maybe I'll meet the man of my dreams," she countered.

"Your boyfriend isn't the man of your dreams?"

Was wringing the man's neck illegal in California? "I meant that figuratively."

"Hmm. So are you game or not?"

"Are you daring me?"

He nodded, his smile unabashedly cocky. "Every day and twice on Sunday. What do you say?"

Why did she have a feeling she was going to regret this? "All right."

He flashed her a heart-stopping smile. "Where do we start?"

Juliette marched over to her desk and withdrew the necessary instructions. She thrust them at Mitch. "Here. Log onto this URL and follow these directions. Come back tomorrow morning at nine."

He ignored the papers in her hand. "Why? You already know 'my type' and the fact I'm a Scorpio. What else could you possibly need to know? That blue is my favorite color?"

He was baiting her; his smile told her that. *Calm, stay calm.* "Just fill out the questionnaire. If you do, it's completely possible that this weekend, you'll have a date with your future wife."

He flashed her those dimples again. "Honey, hook me up with someone I'd actually consider marrying, and I'll write you the biggest endorsement *The Signal* has ever seen."

Juliette took three steps toward him, stopping a mere foot away. Excitement sang in her veins as she pushed the forms into his chest. "You're on."

Early the following morning, Juliette sat in her office, contemplating A Perfect Match's online questionnaire and her answers. A description of her ideal mate jumped off the page: Stable but exciting. Was that an oxymoron? If only she could combine Andrew and Mitch, she'd have the best of both worlds...

She sighed. Certainly, this twenty-something urge for excitement she'd been feeling recently would give way to the more important need for companionship in her thirties and forties. Risky thoughts and behaviors, ones that included Mitch, put her dreams in jeopardy. She wanted stability surrounded by a white-picket fence. Mitch wasn't the kind of man who would be fenced in.

The ringing of the phone interrupted her musings. She lifted the receiver. "Hello?"

"Good morning, darling," Andrew cooed on the other end. "I miss you."

Juliette winced. She'd hardly thought of him all day. "That's sweet of you." She changed the subject. "How's it going there?"

He groaned. "Tedious. The firm my client is trying to acquire has an army of attorneys as tenacious as bulldogs."

"I'm sorry to hear you're having a tough time."

"I hear you're having one, too. Mom told me last night that some jerk at *The Signal* had written a mean-spirited article about your business."

She sighed. This was why she was struggling with Andrew's

proposal; he was so supportive and caring. He was a great friend, but she feared losing him if she turned him down. If she married him, he would always be there for her. He loved small-town stability the way she did. He was good-looking, had a great job, a breezy sense of humor. What wasn't to love?

"The guy is making me insane, and to prove my business isn't smoke and mirrors, I'm supposed to set both of us up on dates. He thinks that will prove I'm a phony."

"It should only prove how brilliant you are."

"You're not worried about me spending the evening with another man?"

He chuckled. "I trust you."

Andrew was so understanding. Why, then, did she feel a vague sense of irritation that he didn't care she'd be having a romantic date with someone else?

"That's one reason I want to marry you, besides the fact I love you," he said. "Have you given my proposal any more thought?"

"This thing with *The Signal* is eating up my mental energy. I can't let this guy ruin my business." She paused, cringing at the sound of Andrew's long sigh across the line. "You're coming back before Christmas. I promise, I'll have an answer then."

Scooping up all his papers from the seat of his truck, Mitch took one last gander at his printed answers to Juliette's questionnaire. Was she serious? Mitch had to wonder. Providing the date and time of his birth was ridiculous, but no big deal. His place of birth was a piece of cake. But some of the other stuff...

People should a) 'say what they mean and mean what they say', or b) express their thoughts and feelings more by use of analogy? What the heck kind of question was that? Bullshit, just like this whole dating experience was going to be.

He could see it now, Juliette's idea of a perfect match for him: a skinny librarian with thick glasses, who'd gleaned her best idea of male anatomy from a text book. He shuddered. Mitch knew his weakness, and it was blondes with curves. Like Juliette.

Man, he was screwed.

Tossing aside his sunglasses, he jumped out of the truck and dragged himself toward Juliette's office. Once inside, the receptionist informed him this portion of the matchmaking process would take an hour or two. He could hardly wait.

Connie buzzed Juliette and informed her of his arrival. She appeared a few moments later, strolling down the hall, toward the reception area. She was dressed in a clinging black dress that ended at mid-thigh, stopping his breath. Silk shimmered around slender legs and lush hips and hugged the curve of her waist.

Mitch started to sweat. Didn't she have any idea that his concentration would go out the window every time he looked at her? Or was that the plan?

"Hi. Is it nine o'clock already?"

"Yeah," he croaked.

She looked at her watch. "Thanks for being on time. Come, sit down. Coffee? Oh, that's right, you don't drink it."

"No, but I'll take some water."

"There's bottled water in the fridge around the corner. Help yourself."

"Thanks." He rounded the corner into the next alcove. Things were starting off semi-well. Better than expected, anyway. Maybe she didn't hate his guts after all. Yeah, and maybe Mother Goose would be America's next president.

When he strode back into the reception area, she motioned him back to her office. He followed her down the hall, watching the beguiling sway of her blonde curls against her shoulders and the way her hips swayed in that dress that hugged her ass. It was going to be a long few hours, indeed.

Once inside her office, he surveyed the place, taking in details he hadn't noticed last time. White walls decorated by simple oils of landscapes in blues, yellows and greens filled his vision. She'd hung a glossy white shelf against one wall and filled it with baffling female knick-knacks like ceramic flowers and heart-shaped picture frames.

Her desk was a large bleached oak number, scattered with papers and a few photos. The first was of Juliette with a redhead a couple years younger.

"Who's your friend?" he asked, pointing to the photo.

"My sister, Kara."

"You wouldn't know it by looking at the two of you."

"We hear that a lot. Why don't you take a seat?"

"Thanks."

He eased into a chair opposite her, and was provided with a view of another corner of her desk, one that had an additional photo. This one showed her with Santa Clarita's home-grown golden boy, Andrew Brimmley. Mitch instantly recognized the tall, bland blond man from *The Signal*'s society pages.

"Is Brimmley your boyfriend?" he asked, trying to sound casual.

"What?" She turned from her computer screen to face him. "Oh, Andrew? Yes."

Her words incited a twist in his gut that Mitch hated to give name to. She'd fallen for a Stanford Law graduate, junior partner at his father's hometown firm of Brimmley, Bedford and Carlisle, and a Rotary Club big wig. What did Juliette see in a poser like that? Would she really marry Brimmley? He was so uptight, it was a wonder he hadn't strangled himself.

Mitch glanced at the picture again. The guy looked like a Ken doll; all tan and dressed in a conservative gray-collared shirt. Mitch frowned. He would never have pegged Juliette to fall for someone stuffy. She seemed too alive to be forced into the stifling box of small town society.

In the picture, taken at a party, Juliette looked great in a turquoise bikini top and black short-shorts. Beside her, Brimmley held her hand.

Mitch glanced away. If he ever got close enough to hold Juliette's hand, he'd be mighty tempted to hold and touch her...and do anything else she'd let him. Correction: everything else she'd let him.

Not a smart thought, MacKinnon. The woman was seeing someone and still the subject of his story. He prayed he could find a leash for his hormones—fast.

"He asked you to marry him, huh?"

Juliette blinked rapidly and looked away. "Yes."

She seemed nervous, self-conscious. Being a journalist—and a man—Mitch probed further. "When's the big day?"

"Actually, I haven't given him an answer yet."

Curiouser and curiouser. And hopeful. "Why is that?"

"That's really not the subject of our meeting. Let's get down to business." She grabbed a pen and the printed copy of his forms. "I've just got a few questions for you."

Mitch would have to be blind, deaf and dumb not to recognize the subject change as an off-putting maneuver, but he vowed they would come back to this subject sooner, rather than later. Call it a gut feeling, but Mitch sensed Juliette was less than thrilled with Brimmley's proposal. The thought made him distinctly cheery.

"What does 'E' stand for?" she asked, interrupting his musings.

What E? "Elvis?"

"Your middle name is Elvis?"

"Hell no!"

She closed her eyes and took a deep breath. "You're impossible. Then what does your middle initial stand for?"

Mitch stifled a groan and cleared his throat. "Uh...I'd rather not say. It's a family name."

"Everything you tell me will be held in the strictest of confidence."

He grinned. "You tell me yours, and I'll tell you mine."

Rolling her eyes, she replied, "It's Rose. That was my grandmother's name."

"Nice," he commented. "Fits well."

"Thank you. Now it's your turn."

Not if he could help it. "This doesn't sound like a professional question. Don't tell me you're going to pair me with a woman whose name rhymes with mine."

She set her mouth into a thin line. "Stop stalling."

He had to give her credit; she was no dummy. Round one to the astrology queen.

"It's Emery, after my uncle in North Dakota. And if you ever repeat it again, I'll—"

"Don't worry." She suppressed a laugh. "Your secret is safe with me."

She whirled her chair around to face her computer screen.

He studied the slender curve of her shoulder, the graceful arch to her back as her fingers flew across her keyboard.

"Damn, you sure can type," he commented.

She nodded, her fingers continuing to tap away at the keyboard. "I put myself and my sister through school by working two secretarial jobs."

He whistled a low note. "That's tough."

"It wasn't easy, but most everyone I knew worked, too. Didn't you?"

He nodded. "During the summer. I had a knee reconstruction my junior year and couldn't work for a while. My parents bailed me out that semester by paying when my athletic scholarship was yanked. The same anyone's parents would have done, I figure."

Mitch saw her shoulders stiffen. Not a good sign.

"Not everyone. The fact you'd think so says a lot about you."

He scowled. "The fact you think otherwise says a lot about you. What gives?"

Juliette tried to pass off his question with a bland shrug. "Just a different upbringing."

"I got that part. It's the details I missed."

"They aren't important."

"You owe me one for the middle name thing. Humor me."

Rolling her eyes, Juliette muttered, "Fine. My mom died when I was twelve. Kara was nine. Dad was never home to know if we needed anything."

Shock crept through his body. "He abandoned you?"

"Nothing that dramatic. He was a slave to the Air Force. Always rising, always ambitious. Rarely home."

Though she tried to play it cool, her mouth was tight, like her folded hands. Mitch felt the strangest urge to embrace her tense shoulders and rub away the hurt. She'd probably slap him if he tried.

"What about friends or neighbors? Who took care of you and your sister?"

"Me. We had never had any friends and didn't know our neighbors, Mr. MacKinnon. We moved ten times in the next six years."

He absorbed her information in thrumming silence. Hers had been a tough adolescence. No wonder she had reacted with distress when he talked about moving as an adventure Friday night. For her, a lonely teenager, moving must have been a terrifying experience.

"I'm sorry," he murmured.

His words hung in the silent aftermath of their conversation. How had they wandered onto such personal ground? It didn't matter, really. But her background gave him a clearer idea of why she was in the matchmaking business: She wanted everyone to have stability, someone to depend on.

That explained why she'd reacted with such venom when he had ridiculed her business in *The Signal*. She'd probably thought he was mocking her dreams and casting darkness on the lonely hearts of Santa Clarita's singles.

No wonder she thought he was an asshole. At the moment, he felt like one.

"Hey, listen..." he began. "I didn't mean for you or the readers to think I regard your business as senseless. If it seemed that way, I'm sorry." He leaned closer, aching to cover her fragile hand on the desk top with his own. He settled for a direct, sincere stare. "Wanting to match lonely people with a compatible someone is a pretty lofty goal."

Her jaw tightened. "Then remember to include that sentiment in your next article, along with an honest assessment of your date."

"You've got my word."

Juliette believed him. The question was, why? Well, his type usually did say what they meant and meant what they said. But even beyond that, his relaxed charm, his straightforward appeal shouted "trust me". Trust a reporter? What a frightening thought.

Aware of his gaze on her, she turned back to her computer screen and picked out pertinent information on his forms. Who would her database pair him with? And why was she dreading an entire evening double dating with Mitch and another woman?

Stupid infatuation! She was supposed to be concentrating on Andrew and his proposal. She shouldn't care, other than for the article, how well Mitch and his date hit it off.

But she did.

Juliette's stomach clenched as she reached for the last page of his questionnaire, the one that asked the applicant to describe his or her ideal mate. When she'd typed hers out last night, the description had sounded less like Andrew than she'd imagined.

Juliette scanned that last page, then turned back to him, frowning. "You didn't fill out the section on your ideal mate."

He shrugged. "I don't know. I haven't met her yet."

Juliette sighed. He probably thought about his future wife as often as Haley's comet made an appearance. "Let's start with what you don't like then."

"All right..." He shrugged. "I don't like women who can't laugh."

"And?"

He paused. "And I don't like smart women who pretend to be stupid because they think that's what guys want."

Juliette paraphrased his dislikes and typed it into the computer. "Anything else? That still leaves a lot of room for error."

Mitch stood. "I'm not real fond of women who try to be guys. You know, the kind who try to bench press more than you at the gym."

She smiled, despite her impatience. "I'm afraid I haven't met that variety."

"They're crawling around the weight machines," he assured in a confidential whisper. "It's frightening to know some of them could kick my butt."

Against her will, she giggled. The man was outrageous! She couldn't help but laugh, wondering if he ever took much of anything seriously.

"Could you to be more specific about your ideal mate, other than wanting a smart and smiling woman who doesn't bench press four hundred pounds? Maybe I should ask you questions."

"Shoot."

"Are you a morning or night person?"

"Definitely morning," he nearly groaned. "I only see midnight on New Year's, and even then it's through bleary eyes."

Juliette nodded. "Me, too. How about smokers? Do you have a preference?"

"Yeah. I don't smoke. I'd kind of like a woman who didn't, either."

She made a note of that. "Describe the activities you like

most."

Mitch cocked his head and paused. Anything that involved getting naked and horizontal with Juliette, he was all for. Damn, he needed to focus.

"Going to a good movie, one with lots of action. Watching sports of almost any kind. Oh, and I love concerts. In fact, I like just about any kind of music." He paused again. "Hanging out with friends and family. I do that most every weekend."

Surprisingly, she and Mitch liked many of the same things. Who would have guessed? "So basically, you like to have fun quietly?"

He nodded. "I'm not into loud parties. A few friends around the pool and the barbecue on a sunny afternoon is my definition of fun."

"Great. How about anything unique. You...mentioned the fact you wanted to see the world. Are you looking for a mate also interested in travel?" She couldn't resist asking. Not that she was personally interested in his answer, of course, but such information was clearly pertinent to his pairing.

"Yeah. I love a woman with a sense of adventure. I had this buddy in college whose girlfriend could throw a few of her belongings in a backpack and travel from Chicago to Oregon, or anywhere else at a moment's notice. I'd love a woman with that kind of spontaneity."

Juliette pursed her lips. Spontaneity? Try instability. Irresponsibility. How could he believe any woman could tend to home and family while traveling America's highways living out of a backpack?

Maybe that was the point. Maybe he just preferred life without ties. That way, he could move on when any arrangement seemed too permanent.

Clearly, Mitch was not her kind of man. So why did she feel

this strange urge to touch him? Why didn't she want to know who in her database might be his perfect match? Undoubtedly because she'd been stupidly indulging in fantasies about the man.

She needed a vacation.

"That should give me enough to start with," she said finally.

Mitch leaned across her desk, closer. "What about you? I don't know anything about you."

And he didn't need to with the vibes running wild between them and their outlooks on life light years apart. "I'm not the one you should be 'getting to know'. Save that for your date this weekend."

"What if I said I was asking for my article?"

Juliette's heart flip-flopped at the sight of his devilish grin and dimples. "I'd call you a liar."

"I can't put anything past you."

"I intend to keep it that way."

Mitch laughed. "I have a question about the survey you gave me. I notice there's absolutely nothing on here about sex."

"Sex?" She nearly choked.

"Yeah. If people are going to have relationships, I presume they're going to have sex."

"I tend to think that if people have enough in common to spend their lives together in harmony, the sexual aspect of their relationship will take care of itself."

"That's a little Pollyanna. Sexual incompatibility could be a serious issue. You should ask people their preference."

"You mean like, are they gay or straight?"

"No. I assume you're running a dating service for heterosexuals. I meant other preferences."

Other preferences? "Like? What would you put, for example?"

"Frequent. And hot. Definitely hot."

Juliette blushed. "You are incorrigible. Now, would you wait outside while I finish inputting the information?"

Mitch sighed and exited her office, closing the door behind him. Juliette found her breathing returning to normal, something it hadn't been since his appearance this morning. The man walked into a room and somehow took up more space than his body occupied. She could almost feel him everywhere in the air.

Maybe she ought to face her infatuation. If she acknowledged it and dealt with it logically, regarded it as a harmless fancy, she could forget it. Maybe she would stop wondering what kissing Mitch would be like, what kind of lover he would be. Anything had to be more effective than pretending she wasn't interested.

In the receptionist's area, Mitch paced. Connie watched him, her brows raised disapprovingly, as if the woman knew he was having lascivious thoughts about her boss.

Damn, Juliette was one sexy woman. Why did she have to be involved with someone else, especially someone like Brimmley, who was as exciting as bologna on white bread?

He stifled a groan. Double dating with Juliette, watching some desperate dweeb trying to put his hands on her... Wow, that visual made him want to break every bone in the imaginary jerk's body.

Drawing in a deep breath, he calmed. No, he wouldn't do that. He couldn't. Juliette was a capable adult. She would handle whatever happened. He just wished he didn't have to watch.

The phone rang. Connie transferred the call to Juliette. Mitch paced.

Juliette's description of her adolescence had shocked him to his toes. How could any man worth his salt put the needs of his career above the needs of his children? No wonder her upbringing had made her wary. The fact she was considering a Rock of Gibraltar like Brimmley for a husband made perfect sense. He didn't need to be a rocket scientist to understand why all his answers about an adventurous woman displeased her.

A moment later, he heard a gasp at the end of the hall.

"Oh my God," Juliette's mutter echoed down the narrow space to the lobby. "No!"

What was happening? Had her phone call brought bad news?

Her personal tragedies were none of his business. But that didn't stop Mitch from darting down the hall. He ignored Connie's stuttering protest for him to stop.

"This can't be," Juliette murmured in a pleading note that gnarled his insides. "It can't."

Giving up all attempts at discretion, Mitch ran down the rest of hallway. He would comfort Juliette, give her a shoulder to cry on. Whatever had happened, he would be there for her.

He pushed open the door of her office, expecting to see her clutching the phone like a lifeline and her eyes brimming with tears. Instead, the phone rested in its cradle. Her eyes were wide with shock in her too pale face.

He dashed across the room and took her cold hands in his. "What is it, honey? What's the matter?"

She glanced at him with huge, uncomprehending eyes. "How did this happen?"

"What? Is someone hurt?"

Juliette swallowed. Some of her composure returned. She met his gaze, then withdrew her hands from his. "No one is hurt. Yet."

He frowned. "I don't understand. What upset you?"

"Take a look at the name of your date," she whispered, then turned away. Over the top of her shoulder, Mitch peered at her computer screen. His name sat at the top in bold white letters. Below that, read the heading *Match's Name.* A few spaces to the right were the words *Compatibility Rating.*

The name and percentage just below that ripped the breath from his lungs.

Juliette Rose Lowell was his perfect match. Their compatibility rating was a cool ninety-three percent.

He laughed. "I'll be damned. Miracles happen after all."

Chapter Four

Juliette lifted her head from her hands, mouth agape. "You think this is funny?"

"Ironic," Mitch corrected, "since the first five days we've known each other have been a tad rocky."

Hence, your computer is berserk and your system is faulty; she knew that was what he was thinking. Well, she couldn't let him. Her business was at stake. She'd worry about the peril to her private life later.

"Maybe the system knows something we don't."

A devilish grin lifted the corners of his lips. "I'm willing to consider that..." he paused, "...after our date."

"Our date" had a scary ring to it. "You know, now that I think about it, the two of us having a date defeats the purpose of this exercise," she backpedaled. "We're both supposed to go out with someone the database matches us with and honestly—"

"We will go out with someone. Each other."

Oh, this was so not good. Of course, Andrew would trust her. Not that she was actually committed to him yet. That wasn't the problem. The issue was, could she trust herself?

"But—"

He held up a finger to stop her words. "No buts. For a truly accurate experiment, we've got to. Supposedly, we have a ninety-three percent chance of lifelong compatibility. Is that right?"

"Ah...yes."

"Well, let's take at least one day to see if that's even remotely possible."

Mitch had her cornered. Juliette began grasping for straws. "Wouldn't you rather meet someone new?"

He leaned close. So close, she could discern gold undertones mixed in the rich brown of his eyes. Juliette held her breath. She closed her eyes, listening to some insidious voice inside her that prayed he would touch her.

"No. Despite our differences, I like you just fine. Now that I've seen your system in action, I'm big enough to admit that your computer might be on to something here. What about you?"

Was he saying that he agreed with the program? How could she answer? The only response that hovered on the tip of her tongue when he was this close—and smelling so damn good—was *I'm dying for you to kiss me.* Very subtle. Not to mention professional, which was how she should be handling this whole escapade. *Think with your brain, not your emotions.*

She sat up and back, removing herself from Mitch's heart-revving proximity. "All right. We'll go out."

"When?"

Lord, he didn't waste any time. Juliette reached for the briefcase behind her desk and withdrew her pocket calendar. "I'm free the second week in January."

"That's six weeks from now, sweetheart. My deadline will have come, gone and grown mold by then. Try again."

He had a point. Besides, putting Mitch off wasn't going to

make him go away. She sighed and focused on the calendar for December. "How about Saturday?"

"That sounds better. So..." His smile turned mischievous. "What shall we do on this date?"

Not go, Juliette thought in panic. If she wasn't careful, Mitch would flash her his heart-melting smile, and she'd fall into his arms. Andrew would be understandably hurt and angry, her best shot at stability and happiness would be gone. Then she'd be left with Mr. Charm, who had already admitted he'd be moving out of town just as soon as someone offered him a better job.

But chickening out would mean leaving her business with a permanent black mark in the eyes of the community.

She sighed, wishing she didn't have such a gift for getting herself into sticky situations.

"I generally recommend to clients that each party plan half of the date."

That elicited his best Cheshire Cat grin. "Really?"

"It's an easy way to learn some of the other person's likes and dislikes, and begin to gauge your compatibility."

"Hmm. I'll have to give our date some thought, then."

That tone... Why didn't he just rub his hands together in glee and make his gloating more obvious? The question was, what did he have in mind? Some X-Games/He-Man sporting event with nine-inches of mud designed to eat her Italian designer pumps? Maybe...but that smile was all about seduction.

She swallowed. Hard.

"Don't plan anything too outrageous."

"Where's your spirit, your sense of adventure?"

"You may have noticed, I try to ignore it."

Grinning, he perched himself on the edge of her desk. "Tsk, tsk, Juliette. What are you afraid of, that you'll enjoy yourself?"

"No, my tastes are just more...mature."

"I'll keep that in mind."

Turning away, Mitch sauntered toward her office door.

"Call me when you've decided on an activity!"

At the door, he turned back. Devilment lurked in his gaze. "Nah, surprises are much more fun."

Juliette dreaded Mitch's last words to her for the next six silent days. Dang it, what was he planning? Over the last few days, her imagination conjured up everything from an X-rated movie to a bowling tournament.

Two could play that game, she decided. Besides, choosing an activity Mitch would loathe might ensure they never got too...cozy. And she knew just the event. Everything in his male sensibilities would rebel. He'd groan, moan, and never want to come within ten feet of her again. She already purchased her tickets online.

Sighing, she rose from her sofa and flipped off the TV she'd been ignoring. Wandering around the living room of her apartment, she peeked out the window, into the parking lot. Kara drove up, returning from her jaunt for ice cream. She scowled, wondering why the girl wanted ice cream in December.

Kara blew in, along with a hearty gust of wind, a few moments later. "I brought you some ice cream." She handed the brightly colored cup to Juliette. "It's chocolate chocolate chip. Your favorite."

"Thanks, but I'm not hungry."

Kara frowned, concern lighting her dark eyes. "I'll put it in the freezer."

Juliette nodded as Kara headed to the kitchen. She knew her sister was only trying to cheer her up. But tonight, she felt too edgy for even the soothing effects of chocolate.

She was letting Mitch get to her more than was strictly smart.

"Okay, passing up chocolate chocolate chip is not like you. What's up?" Kara asked, heading back into the living room.

Juliette sagged onto the sofa, noting it was the same color as her disposition: Blue. "I guess I'm just being moody."

"It's the holidays. You're supposed to be happy."

"I don't feel happy." Juliette shrugged. "Maybe I'm tired."

"Maybe you should let Andrew keep you warm at night, you know?"

"Sex isn't going to solve anything."

"It can't hurt..." Kara frowned. "You and Andrew are... Aren't you?" Something on her face must have shown. "Oh my God, you're not?! He *is* your fiancé."

"Boyfriend," Juliette corrected. "And why is everyone so interested in my relationship with Andrew?"

"Who else has been asking?" Comprehension burst across Kara's pale face. "The reporter, right? He came by last week, didn't he?"

Juliette sighed. "Yes."

"What? Come by or ask questions?"

"Both."

Kara cast her a shrewd glare. "You like him, don't you? That's your problem."

How had Kara guessed? "All right. I admit it. He's...gorgeous and funny. And we have absolutely nothing in common."

Kara grinned. "You're having a hard time getting him out of your mind."

"A terrible time. I don't understand it. Andrew is everything I could ever want. He loves living here. He's going to be a full-fledged partner in the firm soon. We're comfortable together. Why am I hesitating in marrying a man who seems to be everything I want?"

"'Cause he doesn't flip your switch," Kara came back. "Now this reporter—"

"Doesn't flip my switch, either. He just sets off my temper."

"Same difference sometimes. Either way, he gets to you. You're thinking about the guy, right?"

"Yes, but—"

"I'll bet you've imagined kissing him. Am I right?"

Juliette hesitated. "All right, yes, but—"

"Face facts. We don't get to choose who we fall in love with. Andrew may seem to be everything you want. But if you're not interested in him sexually, it could be because something isn't right between you."

"Love? It's just a series of articles. Besides, passion isn't everything. I wonder sometimes if that sweeping, head-spinning variety is something Hollywood invented to sell movie tickets."

Kara shook her head. "No. It's powerful and amazing and once you have it, you'll refuse to settle for less. If you don't have the hots for Andrew, you'd better be asking yourself why."

Juliette's thoughts spun in confusion. Passion seemed important. People who had experienced it said it was vital. She wanted to experience desire, feel the tingle and thrill of being held by someone she couldn't resist, someone who made her heart pound the way Mitch did.

My God, what was she saying? Risk everything for a fling with a guy who had killer dimples? Jeopardize her future so she could feel a few flutters? What she and Andrew had was a better basis for a marriage. It had to be.

Maybe she was deluding herself. Juliette searched deep inside and could only find a yearning that defied explanation.

"Hey." Kara hugged her. "It's going to be all right. You'll figure it out."

Juliette nodded, less convinced than her sister.

"Want to go to the movies with Candy and me to take your mind off of the dilemmas in your love life?"

Love life? Disaster area was closer to the truth. "No thanks. I need to be alone for awhile."

"All right. I'll be home later if you want to talk some more."

She reached for her sister's hand. "Thanks for the ear."

"No problem. Trust me, you'll feel better about all this soon."

Juliette nodded absently, wondering if she would ever feel better now that Mitch had crashed into her life. Maybe if she discovered for herself what he was all about, dissected how they interacted, her libido would understand that they weren't meant for each other in any way, shape or form.

But what if that didn't happen? There was always a chance she would find she liked being with Mitch, that he made her laugh and incited her passion. If that happened, poor Andrew would be devastated. And her future could end in broken-hearted shambles.

So now what?

The Saturday came, the one Juliette had both dreaded and

anticipated. Mitch agreed to pick her up at her apartment at ten that morning. By nine, she had changed outfits three times, fixed her hair twice and cleaned the apartment in-between. At nine-thirty, she was sitting on the sofa, restraining the urge to bite her nails, when the phone rang.

"Hi there," Mitch's voice came across the line.

He was backing out. Juliette's shoulders sagged clear to the floor, as did her spirits. Then she remembered that him canceling was supposed to make her happy. He would be forced to write an article with a conciliatory tone about her business, while her sanity would remain intact.

"Are you canceling?"

"Are you serious? I've been waiting for this." His voice dripped challenge. Great. Why did men have to turn everything, even dating, into some sort of competition?

"Yeah. Me, too," she answered acidly.

"What are you wearing?"

Juliette's jaw dropped. "Is this some kinky question so you can figure out what kind of underwear I wear?"

His chuckle erupted into a full-blown laugh. "No, but good idea. Remind me to ask you again later."

Juliette couldn't help but laugh, too. "You're hopeless."

"My mother would agree with you. Actually, I called because I need you to wear shorts or sweats this morning."

There went the chic red pantsuit she'd bought on impulse yesterday. "Oh? Where are we going?"

"No wheedling it out of me. It's a surprise."

She let out a frustrated grunt. "You never even called to give me a clue. Can't you give me a hint now?"

"Are you going to tell me what you have planned for this evening?" he countered.

"Not a chance. Just bring a suit, a tie, and dress shoes."

"Well, if you won't tell, neither will I. I'll be there in twenty minutes."

Juliette heard a click followed by dial tone. Oh, that man! Andrew would never leave her guessing about their plans. She should have expected the opposite from Mitch. He was infuriating, insufferable...and fun, and attractive. She sank into the recliner near the front door. What was she going to do?

Andrew had called early this morning from Milwaukee. Her whole future seemed uncertain, and all he could think to say was "Hope you slept well" and "Have a nice day". In between a discussion of the weather, of course.

One thing was certain: A day with Mitch wouldn't be "nice". It would either be heaven or hell. She just didn't know which.

Dashing back to her bedroom, Juliette stripped off her pantsuit and jumped into a pair of gray sweats with an aqua-colored sweatshirt. She ripped off her stylish flats and exchanged them for a pair of well-worn athletic shoes. Finally, she tore out the pins holding her elegant French twist in place, then thrust her hair into a ponytail.

Andrew always frowned on "informal" clothing, so Juliette hadn't worn casual much lately. They felt darn good.

She smiled to herself. Then the doorbell rang.

Her smile fell.

He was here? Already? Her pantsuit and all its accessories were lying in the middle of her bedroom floor. Blowing a stray lock of hair from her eyes, she scooped the clothing up in a pile and tossed it in the closet.

Why was she cleaning up? Mitch wasn't going to come within five feet of her bedroom to see her mess. She'd make dang sure of that. And hopefully, Kara would be back this evening when Mitch dropped her off, just to be sure she didn't slip up.

Shaking her head at her mental rambling, Juliette dashed for the door and yanked it open. Mitch stood in the door frame, wearing a dark green T-shirt that accentuated his solid, sculpted chest and a pair of brief black nylon shorts that showcased every inch of his long, muscular legs. She gaped at the light dusting of hair on his calves and hard thighs and swallowed. Even in scrunge clothes, he looked good. Heaven help her.

"What?" he asked in response to her stare. "It's seventy-one degrees this morning. I'd call that shorts weather."

Thanking God he'd misinterpreted her gawking, she dragged her gaze to his face. "It's warmer than I thought."

"I'll wait if you want to change into something cooler."

And relinquish the protective armor of sweat pants? Um...no. "I—I'm fine. Why don't you come in while I finish gathering my things?"

Mitch nodded and stepped inside. "Nice place. Do you live here by yourself?"

She shook her head. "Kara lives with me."

Mitch wandered into the living room and picked up something half-hidden under the sofa. "Who does this belong to?"

He held up the garment with two fingers. A blue lace bra. How could she have missed that in her cleaning? Juliette felt her face heat up. What was it about this man that made her blush?

"That's Kara's." She snatched the undergarment from Mitch, who was trying to hold in his laughter, and rolled the bra into a ball inside her fist.

"Too bad. You'd look good in blue." His heated glance made her insides burn.

Juliette sent him what she hoped he'd interpret as a withering glare. "I'll just...um, put it away."

He grinned. "I'll wait here."

"Have a seat. I'll be back with my stuff so we can get going." She whirled away, vowing to shoot Kara on first sight.

"Actually, point me to the glasses. I brought breakfast."

She turned back and finally noticed a paper bag he carried in one hand. "They're above the dishwasher."

Juliette sped back to Kara's bedroom. Once out of Mitch's eyesight, she tossed the bra on Kara's bed and took a deep breath. Lord, how embarrassing! But that wasn't her real problem. The fact he was imagining her in blue lingerie made her fluttery and hot. That man was damn sexy. How was she going to concentrate on whatever physical activity he had planned for the afternoon when she could scarcely take her eyes off him?

Get a grip, she told herself as she darted to her bedroom and gathered up her hanging bag and make-up case. *Think of this as a business date. Remember this is just a long meeting with varied activities. Be pleasant, but not too friendly, and all will be well.*

Her solution sounded fairy-tale simple. Juliette toted her belongings into the living room and stole another glance at Mitch's back side. With an ass that gorgeous, her whole day was bound to be complicated.

"You like pineapple-mango juice? It's one of my favorites."

She set her bag on the sofa and ambled to the kitchen. "I...ah, never tried it."

He handed her a glass. "It's sweet, but it's fresh-squeezed

from one of my favorite health food stores.”

Juliette nodded and brought the glass swallowed once, twice, then finished half t wonderful.”

He smiled. “I’m glad you like it. I have wh agels and bran muffins, too. They’re all natural,” he added.

“Thanks, but I usually skip breakfast.”

He smiled mischievously. “Today, you’re going to need it.”

What did he have planned, a triathlon? A sex marathon? She blushed at the thought.

“We’re not...ah, going to do anything too strenuous, are we?”

“It will only be as strenuous as you want.”

Maybe he didn’t mean those words as suggestively as they sounded. Maybe it was just her who couldn’t get her brain out of the gutter?

One glance at his devil’s grin he flashed her said otherwise.

Trying to ignore his outrageous flirtation and her hyperawareness of Mitch, Juliette ate half a bagel with some of the marmalade and gulped down another glass of juice. He wolfed down two bran muffins. They departed, Mitch carrying her case and hanging bag. The gentlemanly gesture surprised her.

“Seems strange to be taking luggage along on our first date,” he said with a shrug. “I guess L.A. traffic necessitates strange behavior.”

“We can come back to Santa Clarita to change, if you want,” she offered. “I just thought I’d save us a couple of hours by offering my aunt’s place.”

“It’s a great idea. Frankly, I didn’t know how we were going to...be active all day and make it to whatever you have planned t, otherwise."

They approached a spotless black truck. He opened her door, stored her belongings behind the seat, then helped her up. Even the inside was clean. No McDonald's wrappers like those in Kara's car. And no work-related paraphernalia, which was the case in Andrew's BMW. For a clean nut like herself, his tidiness was a nice change.

He jaunted around to the other door, climbed inside and started the vehicle. He retrieved his iPod from the glove box and hooked it up. "You pick the music. We've got about an hour's drive."

She scrolled through. His selection of music ranged from Nine Inch Nails to Garth Brooks to retro new-wave 80's tunes. Mozart to Motley Crüe. Fats Domino to Daughtry. "You like a little bit of everything?"

He nodded, pulling out onto I-5. "I'm musically schizophrenic."

Juliette laughed. "Kara thinks I'm mentally imbalanced since I can't just choose one genre."

"What does she listen to?"

She set the songs to shuffle and let it play. "Hip hop, if you can believe that."

"I can. My little sister is the same way."

"You have a sister?"

He nodded. "Celia is nineteen going on twenty-eight. She's a freshman at UCLA."

"What's her major?"

"Fashion design." He smiled. "She doesn't want to be anything as boring as a reporter."

Juliette laughed. His sense of humor was so refreshing. Andrew believed life should be taken seriously, not laughed at or through.

"So why did you become a reporter?"

He grimaced. "My senior year of college, I tried to come back to football after rehabbing my knee. I played a few games, but not with the speed I had before." His laugh was sad. "And when you're a wide receiver who hobbles past the line of scrimmage in agony, you're not going to catch many passes."

Juliette resisted an urge to place a comforting hand on his shoulder. His injury had broken a part of his heart. Somehow, she knew that, and she felt guilty for making light of his wounds at their first meeting. Certainly, if someone told her she could no longer play matchmaker for a living, a part of her would die.

"I'm sorry."

He shrugged. "It might have been the best thing that ever happened to me. Guys I went to school with who went on to the NFL are retired now. They're turning thirty and they walk like men twice their age. Me? My knees are in great shape."

The fact he found anything good in such a crushing loss touched a chord of recognition in Juliette. Andrew and Kara both regarded her as hopelessly idealistic.

"I believe all things, good and bad, happen for a reason. We just can't always fathom why when it occurs," she said.

"Maybe so," he finally answered. "Anyway, I wanted to stay as close to sports as possible and I discovered I really liked writing about games. I'm pretty good at it, I'm told, so that helps."

She smiled, battling an insane urge to reach for his hand. "That's great."

He turned to her for a brief moment, his gaze a dark paradox of enticement and embarrassment. "I didn't mean to bring up ancient history. I don't usually bore people with it."

He'd shared something with her. That fact touched Juliette's heart, even as she reminded herself it shouldn't, that Mitch was purely a business contact she needed to impress.

"I'm not bored, I'm flattered," she replied softly.

"You're easy to talk to."

Juliette couldn't find a reply to lighten the intimacy of the conversation. She said nothing.

The rest of the ride passed in companionable silence broken by smatterings of conversation. A short sixty minutes later, they arrived at Venice Beach.

"Here?" she asked, watching Mitch climb out of the truck.

"Absolutely. It's a great place for what I have in mind, not to mention the fact you see the most interesting people."

Reluctantly, Juliette exited the vehicle. In the distance, the water lapped against the pale grains of sand. The weak morning sunlight penetrated the gray fog, taking some of the bite out of the breeze. Between the parking lot and the ocean, a path wound along the shoreline like a ribbon. Beside the trail, a man with cornrows and tattoos listening to a popular alternative band sat in an open-faced hut.

Mitch pulled a blue zippered bag out from behind the seat of his truck, then shut his door. Juliette followed suit, wondering what was inside. Fishing equipment?

"Come with me," he said, trying to repress a smile.

Wondering what he had up his sleeve, she caught up to him.

He touched his hand to the small of her back to guide her forward. A burst of tingles, a sudden awareness, permeated her whole body. Her every sense was attuned to him, his secretive grin, the clean scent of his after shave, the thick, soft texture of his dark hair. She drew in a deep breath, wishing her hormones would go into hibernation. Lord, the way she felt now, she might well pass out if the man kissed her.

They approached the little stand. It sported a fuchsia and neon-yellow striped canvas cover. The small sign, dusted with gold glitter, read *Dreams on Wheels*. Inside, lay dozens of pairs of inline skates.

Juliette's mouth fell open. "This is what you planned? I haven't skated since the eighth grade. Isn't this different than traditional roller skating?"

"I won't let you fall. I promise."

With that, he opened up his carry-along bag and withdrew a pair of black inline skates and thick socks.

"What's your shoe size?" he asked.

"Seven, but—"

"We'll need one pair in a ladies' size seven for the afternoon, please." The long-haired clerk nodded in response, his round John Lennon sunglasses bobbing on his narrow nose.

"No problem, man." He slapped a pair of skates down on the carpeted counter before them. "That's ten bucks."

Mitch quickly paid the man, then grabbed the skates.

Juliette, still trying to wrap her head around this activity, took the skates from Mitch's outstretched hands with reluctance. He turned away and donned his own footwear with wheels. Oh, boy. She didn't remember how to skate, and certainly had never learned this form. It's not that she was likely to injure herself, but...inline skating?

"Mitch," she began. "I know we're each supposed to plan half of this date, but I'm—"

"Not giving this a chance. C'mon. Put them on. You might like it."

He had a point, blast him. Yes, and she shouldn't risk succumbing to closed-mindedness, which would no doubt reflect badly on her business in his follow-up article, even if it meant falling on her rear.

She sighed. "All right."

"Great." Mitch knelt as Juliette bent to untie her shoes. He beat her there and pulled her laces free. As he slid one shoe, then the other, from her feet, then cradled her foot in his hand, her heart raced. What would it be like if he removed the rest of her clothing?

Juliette risked a glance at Mitch—and sucked in a breath. The hot stare of those dark chocolate eyes told her he was wondering the same thing.

Her imagination—and her curiosity—were getting the better of her. Mitch was still her adversary, and she still owed Andrew an answer to his proposal.

"I'll store these in the car while you put on your skates," Mitch said.

Then he glided away, his smooth, male grace evident in just a couple of simple strokes of his legs. Next to him, she'd probably look like she had the coordination of a basset hound.

With a sigh, she put on her rented inline skates.

In the distance, Mitch jogged back through the sand, to the parking lot. When he'd stored her shoes, he headed back toward her. Once on cement again, he displayed the simple elegance of his body, his movements, by simply rolling toward her.

He made skating on these contraptions look so easy. Maybe it was. Maybe she'd blown this whole skating thing out of proportion. She had always been athletic; why not inline skating?

She stood as Mitch swayed toward her, shifting his weight from one foot to the next with the poise of a pro.

When her eyes left the ground, so did her feet. Her backside came within inches of plopping indignantly on the concrete until Mitch lunged forward and caught her beneath the arms before impact.

Helping her up, he asked, "You okay?"

She gave him a shaky nod. "I think so. Thanks."

Still, his arm lingered around her, and Juliette's courage increased with his support. She took her gaze away from the frightening firmness of the cement and made the mistake of looking into his melted dark eyes.

"I'll be happy to rescue you anytime."

She should discourage his suggestive tone and train of thought, get her balance and ask that he release her. Those would be the actions of a smart woman. Unfortunately, she wasn't always wise, and now, she couldn't seem to find her tongue.

Mitch smelled good, naturally manly, not like that heavy citrus cologne Andrew wore. His hair was attractively disheveled, not overly sprayed. And his body...

Why couldn't she stop comparing Mitch and Andrew? They were different men, apples and oranges, brawn versus brains. Comparisons were pointless.

Oh, but one small step, and she'd really be in his arms, against that hard chest. Would he kiss her with passion, real passion?

She'd been putting off physical intimacy with Andrew for reasons she didn't want to examine too closely. Andrew, bless him, had written it off to ladylike restraint. Juliette felt anything but ladylike and restrained around Mitch.

Balling her fists, she stepped away from him. She had to remember the facts: Sexual chemistry didn't mean she and Mitch would have a good relationship. Despite what her program said—and there had to be an error in the data somewhere to produce such a faulty result—she and Mitch weren't compatible. She and Andrew were. All she had to do was say yes, then she and Andrew would be man and wife. Then the stability she'd always wanted would be hers. Comparisons and a racing pulse were only destructive to her future.

But if she didn't keep some distance between herself and Mr. MacKinnon, remember this was purely a business date, she feared she'd succumb to temptation and find all about sexual chemistry in Mitch's arms.

Chapter Five

Juliette tiptoed away from Dreams on Wheels, pensive and silent. What had he done to upset her? Mitch wondered. He'd merely kept her from falling...and held on too long, looked into her eyes while praying for some sign of interest. To a woman almost engaged, that was probably too strong too fast. But she didn't exactly inspire monk-like behavior.

Then he'd found curiosity in her breathless stare. The urge to kiss her had been like a two-ton weight on his chest. Even now, he was still cursing the fact that running shorts didn't hide his reaction to Juliette too well.

Despite all that, he reached out to touch her. Swearing beneath his breath, he yanked his hand away before he made contact.

She was almost engaged, damn it, to an up-and-coming attorney who had the personality of a sappy radio deejay crossed with Dr. Phil. For the life of him, Mitch didn't know how to compete with Andrew Brimmley for the fair Juliette. The man was as stable as gravity, and Mitch suspected that was Juliette's primary attraction to him. Not that it should matter since, strictly speaking, they were here for business reasons.

Unfortunately, Mitch found himself wanting to compete with Brimmley—and win.

Andrew's whole life centered around a social circle that

reeked of pretentiousness. Uptight described them, and Juliette didn't fit in that realm. Maybe the fact she hadn't answered Brimmley's proposal meant that, deep down, she knew she didn't belong with a stuffed shirt like Andrew.

Mitch also had this story to consider. Duty bound him to evaluate Juliette's company, their compatibility and chemistry, then analyze the effectiveness of her crazy methods. Doing that with any kind of objectivity would be next to impossible with his hormones running wild.

Down boy, down, he admonished himself and followed her at an easy glide.

Now what? "So, Juliette, do you enjoy your business?"

She turned to him, struggling to stay on her feet. "I wouldn't stay open if I didn't think it was both fun and productive." She sent a sidelong stare his way, peering against the anemic sunlight. "There's someone for everyone. I can help anyone willing to help themselves find a special mate."

"You seem very passionate about A Perfect Match."

"I am." She tucked a lock of stray hair behind one ear. The gesture looked almost self-conscious. "I got the idea from watching my mom. She spent so much time alone with us kids, always waiting for Dad to come home. She and Dad married young. She never said so, but I think if she had known Dad's priorities in life would be work first and family last, she would have thought twice about marrying him."

"Would you marry a man like that?"

Without pause, she shook her head. "I watched Mom pine for him. It was painful. Then I discovered firsthand what waiting for him was like after she died."

Don't ask. Don't do it, he admonished himself, then asked anyway. "You think Brimmley will put his home life before his law practice?"

She jerked her head around to meet his gaze—and fell toward the ground.

Again, he caught her before her attractively curved derriere hit the pavement. As he wrapped his fingers around her waist, a burst of tingles shot up his arm. A masochistic side of him gripped her just a little more tightly. What was it about Juliette? He couldn't start thinking of her as a story and stop thinking about her as a woman.

"Are you all right?" He sounded like he'd been through a two-hour workout.

"Fine." Her breathless reply shivered up his spine.

Mitch helped her stabilize, then he slowly forced his fingers to disengage and released her. "I'm sorry. Your relationship is none of my business."

"Thank you." She adjusted her sweatshirt over her lush breasts. Mitch swallowed—hard.

He focused on her face before his reaction to her body became really noticeable. "It's just that prying is my life."

A reluctant smile tugged its way across her face. "You're good at it."

"I try. Do you...want some help until you get the hang of inline skating?"

"I think I'm getting it," she demurred.

Moments after her assurance, her feet darted out from underneath her. Juliette struggled to find balance, her legs kicking out before her like a tap dancer's.

Mitch put his arm behind her shoulders to steady her, and Juliette regained her balance.

"I guess I do need a little help."

He rolled behind her, placing a hand on each shoulder. Her ponytail had come loose, and a mass of golden curls lay across her back. Mitch inhaled some exotic scent reminiscent of tropical oils and fruits. He forgot what he'd planned to say.

"I'm standing. Now what do I do?" she asked.

"Ah...first of all, inlines are more like ice skates than the old-fashioned skates with four wheels. These wheels are in a row in the middle of the skate, the way a blade would be on an ice skate."

"I noticed," she replied dryly.

"The trick is strong ankles and good posture. Try it. I'll stay behind you."

Juliette made a tentative push-off and stayed erect. Mitch gently pulled her shoulders back over her hips. "Watch your alignment. Getting off balance is the worst thing you can do."

She nodded and pushed off on the other foot, back straight. This stroke was smoother.

"Better, but bend your knees," he encouraged, skating to her side. He clasped her elbow to lend support. "Keep going."

Within ten minutes, she had mastered the basics. She skated by his side, taking in the scenery and beach vendors in makeshift booths around them, selling everything from art to palmistry. He concentrated on Juliette's smile of delight. God, she looked...incredible. Sexy, feminine, quietly strong.

"Look," she called out, pointing at a group of people standing in a circle. In the middle were a couple of teenage boys gyrating on their skates to the thump of hip-hop music.

One of the kids did a flip in mid-air. Juliette gasped. "Did you see that?"

The smile in her eyes lit a spark in his body. Did the uptight Andrew Brimmley ever see this expression of wonder cross her peaches and cream face? Ever see her flush with excitement? He didn't want to think so. The vision of Juliette in

Brimmley's bed made him want to hit something, namely the man's face.

"Cool, huh?" he replied.

"Let's get closer."

Mitch followed as she skated toward the circle. Right now, if she'd asked for the moon, he would have tried to give it to her. What did that say about his feelings for the almost-engaged Miss Lowell?

That he needed to back off fast, only he wasn't sure how and didn't want to. *Real professional, MacKinnon.*

When he reached her side, she stood on the outer fringes of the circle, clapping her hands to the rhythm of the music blaring from the portable stereo. Her infectious grin had him smiling.

"Do you see this often down here?"

He shrugged. "Pretty much."

She stared at one of the boys dancing in the center, despite his baggy shorts. "I wish I could do that. It looks like fun."

"We can come out here again, if you want. I'll see to it you learn."

She bit her lip shyly. In the next instant, Juliette's fingers touched his elbow, and not for balance. Mitch reached for her hand, amazement surging through his body. Did she feel something for him beyond annoyance? She couldn't ignore the strong chemistry thrumming between them, right?

"Thanks for putting up with me, I know I gave you a hard time about skating and all, but—"

He waved her words away. "Don't worry about it. I didn't want to go my first time, either."

Her bright smile held both gratitude and flirtation—and nearly knocked him to his knees.

Spending a day with the lovely Juliette was fast becoming more gratifying than it should be. The fact she seemed to enjoy his company only added to the pleasure, made her harder to resist.

After the circle of skaters broke up, Juliette drifted away from the crowd, further down the cement path. Mitch followed. Without thinking, he reached for her hand.

When had simple hand holding become so significant? He was a guy, and like most others, getting laid was cause for a smile. But as much as Mitch wanted Juliette—and that was a whole big bunch—he wanted her to like him more. Sex could wait.

Had he really just thought that? Yep. And even more, he meant it.

Maybe, just possibly, Juliette's computer program had selected them as a perfect match because it was true.

Juliette's heart tangled up in the swell of emotion lodged in her chest as Mitch's fingers wrapped around hers.

She caught sight of his stare in her peripheral vision and turned to meet it. His gaze probed, deep, meaningful, unflinching. He wanted more than to hold her hand...but he didn't press. Oh, God. She wanted the same thing. Did that mean her relationship with Andrew was defective? These feelings matched her reluctance to wear his ring and her increasingly cold feet.

Only spending the day with Mitch, like any uncommitted woman might, would prove her theory one way or another. Besides, hadn't they agreed their compatibility rating of ninety-three percent deserved at least one day to test?

Was she rationalizing her desire for someone she shouldn't want?

"Are you ready for lunch?" he asked suddenly into their thick silence.

She wasn't hungry after eating an unaccustomed breakfast, but if he was... "Sure. What did you have in mind?"

"Ming Waters." He chuckled. "It sounds much classier than it is."

She couldn't stop her grimace. "It sounds like Chinese."

"It is. You don't like it?"

"I don't like anything I can't identify,"

He burst out laughing. "Now you sound like my little sister. She's barely progressed from the peanut butter and jelly sandwich stage."

"My tastes are a little more adult than that."

"You tempt me to put those words to the test," he murmured.

Her face heated up with a blush again. She punched his arm playfully to cover up her red face. "I meant food."

He shrugged innocently. "So did I."

"And I'm Santa Claus."

Mitch spun in front of her and skated backward, then reached a hand toward her chin. "Your beard is looking a little thin, Kris."

She swatted his hand away with a smile. "Stop clowning around."

"Why? It's what I do best."

She rolled her eyes. "I noticed."

"So you'll be adventurous and try Ming Waters?"

Did she have much of a choice against his persuasiveness? Around him, trying new things seemed like the norm. "Let's go."

They skated another quarter of a mile, then turned up a

dingy side street. On the corner sat a squatty ancient building. Its warped paint looked as if it had been yellow in a previous century, though she couldn't tell for sure.

"I told you it's a real classy place," Mitch joked.

"Gosh, is it even up to health codes?"

"The inside is spotless," he assured her. "The food is heavenly. Trust me, and I'll order you something you recognize."

She shot him a skeptical glance. "All right."

Mitch opened the door, then skated inside behind her. Though the dining area was no bigger than the average fast food restaurant, it appeared larger. Sunlight filled the interior via huge windows all around. Pristine white paint covered every wall, along with cheery bamboo baskets. A wallpaper border depicting a boy carrying a rice cart wrapped around the dining area for a more cultural feel.

And the place was packed with everyone from beach bums to upscale couples.

"If you'll find us a table, I'll go order." He gestured to the counter up front.

Nodding, Juliette turned away and spotted a trio of folks leaving. She slid into their booth and watched as a young blond man with three earrings cleaned off the table.

A few minutes later, Mitch arrived with a tray bearing six plates, three bowls and two cups.

"Good God, how many people are coming to lunch?"

He laughed. "Just us."

Shaking her head in amazement, she replied, "We'll never finish."

"We'll see." He pushed a plate in front of her. "This is lemon chicken. It contains exactly what you think, chicken in a light lemon sauce."

"What's all this stuff?" She pointed to the goop on another plate he set before her.

"Lo mein. It's just noodles, peas and soy sauce. Nothing too hard to identify. Take a bite."

Gingerly, Juliette poked her fork into the noodle-vegetable concoction, took up a bite and put it into her mouth. She expected to hate the stuff. It sure smelled funny.

"Decent?" he asked.

"Surprisingly, yes."

"Good. Try the chicken."

Feeling a little braver, she stuck her knife and fork into the meat and sliced off a bite. Tangy, tart, tender, sweet.

"Oh, that's really good."

Smiling, he reached for his chopsticks. "I hate to say I told you so, but..."

"I know. You told me so." She rolled her eyes and laughed.

Between bites of some chicken and vegetable mixture, he asked. "Now that I'm not the enemy anymore, are you going to tell me what you have planned for tonight?"

"Who said you weren't the enemy?" she shot back. "Are you planning to write a complimentary article about my business?"

"If I did, I'd pretty much have to write that you and I are compatible, maybe for life."

"Not necessarily," she hedged. "Couldn't you write that we had a pleasant time that might have led to something more substantial if our circumstances had been different?"

He lowered his chopsticks and leveled her a direct stare. "Is that true?"

Juliette swallowed the lump of chicken suddenly stuck in her throat. "I'm having a great time."

"No, the other part. The something more substantial." He leaned forward, closer, and whispered. "If it wasn't for Brimmley, would you see me again?"

What could she say? That the more time she spent with him and his off-beat sense of humor, the more she appreciated him? Maybe an equally succinct answer would be that each time he looked at her, she longed to experience the dark heat behind his gaze, to feel it from his hands on her skin. She sighed. Why had he asked this question, anyway? Curiosity or, heaven help her, real interest?

Juliette leaned back in her booth seat, away from the intimacy of their proximity. "I...haven't given it much thought. I suppose anything is possible."

"But what about probable? If I write an article endorsing your business, I'm essentially saying that I believe we could spend a lifetime together without snarling our way through it. How do you feel about our chances of that?"

An endorsement from him after his first review of her business would go a long way toward reviving her reputation. Maybe the phone would start ringing again.

But she didn't want to answer him, didn't want to examine too closely the feelings she was having for Mitch. She'd never been a coward, but that prospect was too scary.

He was going to leave Santa Clarita, probably sooner than later. If she allowed herself to feel something for him, he would leave her behind to mend her broken heart alone. If she married Andrew, the answer to this question would be moot. But Mitch's intense stare demanded a reply now.

She cast her gaze down at the faux-wooden Formica table and watched her fingers curl with tension. "We'll never know. The only way we could discover the truth is to spend more time together."

He smoothed his hand across her cheek, then curled it around her jaw, lifting her gaze to his. "I was thinking the same thing."

They finished their lunch and skated back to the truck in thoughtful silence. Juliette's anticipation for the coming evening warred with her common sense as Mitch drove them away from the beach.

As they sped down Pacific Coast Highway, the sun broke through the clouds in a glorious burst. She stole covert glances at Mitch's strong profile. A thoughtful crease on his forehead and the downturn of his mouth shouted deep thought. Not to mention the long, heated stares he tossed in her direction at every stop light.

"Where to now?" he asked, breaking the silence.

"My aunt's house is in Santa Monica, off I-10. Like I told you on the phone, she won't be home, but she said we could use her place to change for this evening."

He simply nodded.

No joke? No teasing comment? How unlike Mitch.

Juliette attempted to lighten the mood. "Aren't you going to ask me where we're going tonight?"

"If I do, will you tell me?"

"No."

The traffic light before them turned red. Mitch stopped and faced her. "Then I won't ask."

Breathing became increasingly difficult as Mitch's rich, dark gaze slid over her face and down her body.

"Besides, I like the anticipation of not knowing what will happen next."

His tone, deep and suggestive, told her this evening's plans were about the last thing on his mind. And for some reason, the longer he looked at her, the less important the tickets in her make-up case became. Good God, maybe she was in over her head with Mitch.

Or falling head over heels.

Half an hour later, they arrived at her aunt's tiny beach apartment. True to Aunt Maggie's form, the place, right down to her 1970s tan and gold throw rugs, was spotless. Thanking God some things in life were constant, Juliette pointed Mitch to the fresh towels and the guest bedroom. She was achingly aware that he waited to close the door until she'd disappeared into Aunt Maggie's room.

Five minutes later, she heard the shower running. The spray of water she heard pounded her with the fact that only one tiny door separated her from Mitch's hard, naked body. And she suddenly resented that door.

She had never, ever had thoughts like this about Andrew. Not once. That was the problem. Mitch set her hormones on full alert, and she had no idea what to do about that lamentable fact.

Why didn't she feel this way about Andrew? Want him so bad that she felt fixated? It was so darned inconvenient to feel this rush of desire for the wrong man. After all, he would never understand her concept of security and happiness.

Morosely, she slipped into her warm bath water, wondering how this evening would end. Somehow, Juliette couldn't see concluding their date with a simple handshake. Not when they both wanted so much more.

Her simple business date would definitely wind up completely personal if she didn't stop that train of thought. The problem was, Mitch seemed to encourage it with his sizzling stares and whispered confidences. And she wasn't exactly beating him off with a stick.

She had to get a grip. Indulging in a fling, although pleasurable, with a man who had values completely opposite from her own was stupidity. It was inviting heartbreak.

After washing up and slipping from the tub, she put a few curls in her hair and refreshed her make-up at her aunt's vanity. Next, she slipped into her favorite after-five dress, a low-cut blue velvet number with a skirt that ended two inches above the knee.

Knowing she shouldn't care if Mitch liked it or not, Juliette slipped out of her aunt's bedroom and wandered nervously into the living room. There, she found Mitch wearing a navy blue suit that accentuated the lean lines of his body and a crisp white shirt, minus a tie.

He tossed her a casual glance, then did a double take, his jaw somewhere in the vicinity of his feet. "Holy..." He swiped a hand through his damp hair, his eyes glued to her. "Wow. You look incredible."

"Thanks." She tried not to blush again as she returned his compliment—hard not to when his broad shoulders filled out his suit coat to perfection. "You look great, too."

Clearing his throat, he reached for a gold-framed picture to his right. "So, is this you and your sister?"

Juliette peered closer and wanted to die of embarrassment. "We'd decided we'd make great pop singers, even though we were only kids. My Aunt Maggie made the costumes when we stayed with her that summer."

"You look fabulous, dahling," he teased.

She smiled self-consciously. "For us, anything brief and silver lame was *it*."

"Looks like fun." He set the picture down on the antique sewing machine and held up three neckties. "I brought a few ties. I wasn't sure which would match best. Would you, ah...mind helping me out?"

Juliette looked the ties over. She settled on one comprised of blue, gray and red flecks. "Definitely this one."

Mitch tossed the other two in his duffle bag, which lay by his feet. "Thanks."

After a lingering stare, he turned to the mirror above the sewing machine and proceeded to knot the tie around his neck. The first attempt ended up lopsided. After the second try, the stylish tie hung nearly to his hips. Mitch let out a frustrated grunt.

Juliette couldn't help but laugh.

"If you're so much better at tying this thing, come do it."

"I am and I will."

With an impish smile, she stepped in front of Mitch. And stopped when she realized her body was just a breath from his. Big mistake. A muted woodsy scent penetrated her senses, infusing her with a rush of awareness.

She raised her stare to his. Another stupid move. Dark demand flared in his eyes. The wide set of his shoulders and his clenched jaw told her he was restraining himself. That would end with the slightest whisper of encouragement from her...

Swallowing, she reached for the tie. Her fingers brushed his chest. Their hand-holding earlier today was much further down the pleasure scale than this close contact.

He inhaled sharply. Juliette felt his inhalation, sucked in his vitality, smelled his maleness and want. He infused her with an electric surge of desire.

Oh God, she'd never felt this way in her life.

She lifted the tie and knotted it, as she used to do for her father. Her fingers trembled. Mitch grasped her arms as she finished, bringing her inches closer.

"I want to kiss you senseless."

Please do!

Juliette inhaled a ragged breath. "Mitch…please."

"Please what?" he whispered. "Let you go? Or kiss you?"

She closed her eyes and prayed for strength. "I can't do this. I'm involved…"

"And it's a damn shame." His velvety murmur slid over her, shooting tingles up her spine. "But you didn't answer my question. Tell me what you want."

Juliette grasped onto honesty when nothing glib came to mind. "This doesn't make any sense. The direction we want our lives to take is so different."

"But what we want out of life right now is the same."

Fighting an urge to press her lips to his, mere inches away, and give into the passion, she closed her eyes. "I—I just can't."

He released her. "Tell me if you change your mind."

Had she been granted a reprieve or been rejected? Both feelings swirled through her in a confused ache as she grabbed her bags and fled for the door.

Juliette gave directions to the next part of their date in monosyllables. That suited Mitch just fine.

He would never have thought two people could create such invisible fireworks on one damned date. He gripped the wheel tightly. Still, his hands trembled with an insane urge to touch her. Did she know that? Feel it, too?

More important, he ached to know if her "I don't know" would ever become a "yes".

Forty-five minutes later, he parked in front of the Shrine Auditorium. The signs out front advertised the American Ballet Theater's rendition of *The Nutcracker.*

He groaned. "The ballet?"

Juliette turned to him, biting her lip. "I'm afraid so."

A four-letter curse slipped out of his mouth before he could stop it.

"*The Nutcracker* is so festive. It seemed like a good idea."

"Yeah, when you were mad at me."

"Well...yes. But I've always wanted to go."

Mitch shot her a challenging stare. "The Boy Scout hasn't taken you?"

"Too loud for Andrew," she admitted.

He could one-up Brimmley and make Juliette happy by doing nothing more than sitting in a padded seat and watching people dance for a few hours?

"Then we'll go." He brushed back a curl from her cheek. "And since you kept such an open mind about skating, I'll try to do the same during this...event."

Juliette smiled gratefully. At that moment, Mitch would have given her his right arm if it would have made her happy. And why was that?

He knew he should back off, find objectivity. Damned difficult when her bare shoulders snared his gaze and her every glance tugged at his heart.

"Thank you," she whispered with a soft smile.

He grabbed her hand and wrapped his fingers around her delicate ones. With a squeeze, he said, "I like seeing you smile. Come on."

Together, they climbed out of the truck and headed for the

auditorium, hurrying to escape a chilly evening breeze. Once inside, they strolled to the bar to await curtain. Juliette ordered white wine, Mitch a beer.

He held up his bottle. "Let's toast...a great day with some damn fine company."

With a shaky nod, she tipped her glass against his. "Here, here."

For the next half an hour, Mitch engaged her in all manner of small talk, everything from community development to current entertainers. Juliette said little, and Mitch suspected he'd gotten too close at her aunt's place and spooked her.

A glance at her taut profile told him she was downright nervous.

"You okay?" he asked.

She met his gaze. Mitch absorbed the fear in her blue eyes.

Fear? That something would happen between them? An instant later, she jerked her gaze to the floor, and he knew. Yes, she was afraid something would happen.

She was also afraid she wouldn't have the will to stop it.

Suppressing a rush of jubilation, he suggested they take their seats. With a murmur, Juliette agreed.

Twenty silent minutes later, the show started. Mitch planned to close his eyes and plot a new strategy for exploring whatever was going on between himself and the beguiling Miss Lowell. Curiosity kept them open.

The curtain went up and a group of dancers came on stage, depicting a holiday party comprised of several families. A ten-foot Christmas tree on rollers took a corner downstage.

Women pirouetted, men leapt. Mitch gaped. "Good Lord, those men are wearing pants so tight, I can guess their religion."

"Shhh," came the admonition from a couple beside him.

Juliette bit her lip to repress a laugh. "You're terrible."

"It's true," he defended.

Within fifteen minutes of leaps, lifts and turns, Mitch had to admit that, although the dancers weren't playing a sport, they were incredibly well-trained athletes.

But more fascinating was Juliette's face. Flushed and wide-eyed. Captivating as the dancers enthralled her. She smiled; she frowned. Delight shone in the glow of her cheeks, mimicking Clara's delight when her nutcracker turned into a prince.

He'd never seen Juliette more beautiful, and all because she radiated happiness.

God, he'd sit through two days of the ballet to keep this look on her face. Even better, he'd love to put that look there himself.

Disappointment sliced through him when the lights rose and the curtain fell for intermission. Another wave of discontent washed over him when she excused herself to the rest room.

He took the opportunity to look at the others around him. Cultured and sedate described the crowd well. Good-looking women abounded. Too bad he hadn't known that sooner, before Juliette. After spending an evening with her, he wasn't really interested in anyone else.

Whoa! That kind of thinking was bound to get him in hot water. But he wasn't turning that faucet off. He had a chance with Juliette. Yes, it was a small one. Professional or not, he intended to take full advantage of it for two simple reasons: One, Andrew Brimmley was nowhere near her Mr. Right. And two, he could never remember being this crazy about a woman. Any woman.

Even better, Juliette wasn't immune to him, either.

Chapter Six

"What did you think of the ballet?" she asked once they had returned to the truck and headed for the freeway.

"Fascinating."

"Did you really think so?" She rushed on, turning to face him in the truck. "I thought it was great. So elegant and romantic."

He sent her a smile, complete with dimples, that melted her insides. "Surprisingly, it wasn't awful."

"Did you get over having to look at the male dancers in their tights?" she teased.

"I'm blocking that part out and making a mental note to tell my mother not to buy me any for Christmas."

"Why? You'd look great."

"I would, huh?"

Oh, very smart. Let Mitch know she had noticed his body. Maybe she should just hold up a ranking between one and ten to let him know how she really felt.

"I...ah. It was a joke. Bad one. I know you wouldn't wear them." She smiled, hoping it didn't look as stiff as it felt.

Juliette also stared at the strong angles of his face. Had she ever wanted to touch a man's jaw before? Not to her recollection, and never this badly.

"Not without a *very* enticing incentive, which I'm not counting on tonight. So, where are we going now?"

If she didn't watch herself, she'd be offering him that incentive. "Have you heard of Mama Leone's?"

He nodded. "Never been, though."

"It's wonderful Italian food." She closed her eyes and sighed. "The best, at least the one time I ate there."

"I'm for anything that makes a woman sigh like that."

Again, that suggestive note, the one that had been driving her crazy half the day. As before, his deep velvet voice started a warmth in her stomach and turned her knees to mush. Juliette lapsed into protective silence. She was tempted to find out if he was the one, the man who could make her sigh, for very different reasons. Yet the thought of Mitch trekking like a vagabond through life—and breaking her heart—stopped her.

In twenty minutes, they'd crested the hill and descended into the San Fernando Valley. After crossing Sepulveda, they stopped at Mama Leone's. Despite the fact they were ten minutes early for their 10:30 reservations, the dignified, gray-haired maître d' seated them right away.

Unfortunately, he seated them in a cozy candlelit corner behind the fountain, away from the other diners, a mere ten feet from the romance of the roaring fire. A dreamy mural of the canals in Venice filled the wall to her right. Green plants abounded and a low, sexy ballad whispered from the overhead speakers. She wondered what kind of ideas this atmosphere would give Mitch. Hopefully not the same kind she was having.

Why had she suggested they come here? The sumptuous Italian food had lingered in her memory; the ambiance, created for lovers, had not, despite the fact she'd come with Andrew before. What impression would her choice of eateries leave on Mitch?

"I, ah... This isn't what I had in mind. We can leave if you want." Her smile was hopeful.

Mitch's gaze canvassed the room. His brows creased into a perplexed frown. "This place looks perfect to me. The food looks fattening." He gestured to the menu the waiter had left. "But my arteries can handle one evening of fat."

"We can always head for home and drive through In-and-Out Burger."

"No way, lady. You look too stunning for a burger joint, much less a drive-thru. And the fat content would be just as bad."

Great. She had to sit here for the next hour, at least, watching the fire reflect off the healthy glow of his face and darken the shade of his rich brown eyes... Not to mention staring at his lips, wondering, almost aching, to find out how they felt against hers...

She affected a yawn. "Gosh, aren't you tired? We've had such a big day—"

"Juliette, stop." He pinned her with a starkly honest stare. "I'm not going to jump you, and a crackling fire and pretty murals aren't going to give me any ideas I haven't already had."

She felt a flush crawl up her cheeks. He was certainly direct. And part psychic. He had a good point, however. They were in public, and he wasn't going to attack her like a rabid animal.

Juliette opened her mouth to reply. Thankfully, their waiter came around to take their drink orders, instead. She regrouped mentally while asking for a glass of merlot.

The moment the slick-haired waiter departed, Juliette changed the subject. "So, have you made up your mind what you're going to write in your next article about A Perfect Match?"

He cocked his head to the side in consideration. "I've been thinking about it since we discussed it at lunch, actually. I keep coming back to one point. Maybe you can help me out."

Mitch's words were innocent. His smile was not. Lord, the man must have earned his Ph.D. in flirting. Without laying a hand on her, he was talented enough to send her into heavy breathing.

"You want my help?"

"Oh, yeah. What are you offering?" His grin widened.

"Seriously," she chastised, folding her hands in her lap.

"Seriously. I can't decide at what point I could honestly declare that we're a perfect pair. Most couples date before deciding that."

"We have," she protested.

"Once," he countered. "Other couples talk, get to know each other."

She had the feeling he was leading her down some primrose path that would lead to a pile of thorns. "We've done some of that that today, too."

"To a point, but most couples also get to know each other...more intimately."

Juliette fell silent and shifted uncomfortably in her chair. A retort that she and Mitch must be the exclusion to that rule sat on the tip of her tongue. She couldn't quite bring herself to say it with visions of passionate arms and tangled sheets clouding her judgment. She inhaled raggedly.

She couldn't figure out why he affected her so deeply, stirred all the heated fantasies of damp skin and slow caresses she'd ever had. He was only destined to leave her for greener pastures.

"What is that old wives' tale?" he continued. "Something

about the magic of a first kiss. They say a person can tell at the moment their lips meet another's if you have that chemistry. You think that's true?"

Feet fidgeting, Juliette avoided his gaze. "I never gave it much thought."

And she couldn't let herself think about it now.

"Maybe you should."

Her head snapped up. Their gazes met, his direct, challenging. Heat and promise emanated from the depths of his dark eyes. Some wild part of her responded to him on such an elemental level, she considered finding the nearest dark corner to explore his embrace.

Sanity put the brakes on her runaway thoughts. "We shouldn't have this discussion. And you shouldn't be trying to extort kisses out of me."

Mitch grasped her hand. "I'm not extorting, merely making a point. I'm also wondering what you're afraid of. Nothing will happen between us that you don't want."

Looking at Mitch, Juliette found there was very little from him that she didn't want. Couldn't he understand that speeches like that essentially offered her temptation wrapped in silk sheets, scented with testosterone? She had to stop thinking like this, for her sanity, for her future. He had to understand that she couldn't get involved with a grass-is-greener type of man.

Yet she tried to picture Andrew as her groom, but she could only grasp a fuzzy, gray image. Biting her lip, she told herself that clouded vision stemmed from nothing more than a physically tiring day. It couldn't mean anything else. In two hours, she'd be safe and sound in her bed, very much alone.

"If you want to end this date with a handshake, I totally understand that," he continued, leaning closer. "But I'd be lying if I said I didn't want more."

Juliette withdrew from his grasp and lowered her gaze to the table, battling an insane urge to crawl across its red-clothed surface and kiss him breathless. Such crazy impulses for a man destined to leave her didn't speak well for her resistance.

"Just do me a favor," Mitch continued. "Tell me why I make you nervous."

Her gaze flew to his. How was she supposed to answer that, without leading him to a false conclusion that her feelings of attraction meant something more significant than they should? "I can't explain it."

Coward, she chastised herself. Maybe if she told him the truth about her weakening resolve, he'd take pity on her and leave her be. Yeah, and the Christians probably thought the same thing about the Romans before they unleashed the lions.

"Try. I just might understand."

She owed him that much since he'd been incredibly decent and open-minded today. "It's just that...you and I are so..." She twisted her napkin around her hands. "Well, we're...different."

"No two people are the same," he shot back.

"No. *Really* different."

"Ahh." He nodded as if comprehension had dawned. "You're convinced we want different things from life. It's that stability thing again, isn't it?"

She inhaled nervously and nodded. "That about sums it up."

"You know, I think you have the impression I'm anti-commitment. That's not at all true," he said. "I would love a woman who lives for fun and family the way I do."

""That's not likely to happen if you move every month."

He frowned. "I'd take my wife and kids with me."

She gaped at him in open-mouthed shock. "You can't

expect your family to readjust to a new town whenever the urge strikes you to pack up and go. Just because you're interested in scouting out every zip code in America doesn't mean the rest of the family would be."

"Every zip code? I think you're overreact—"

"I've been through this most of my life," she interrupted, gathering steam. "New schools, new people, new houses. And just when one became comfortable, Dad told us the time to leave had come again. It's a lousy, irresponsible way of life, one you shouldn't expect anyone to share with you."

"Wait a minute," he protested. "It's not as if I do this on a whim. Well, at least not anymore. I move for better jobs, which is a kind of security in itself. What's wrong with that?"

She sighed in frustration. "You see, this is why we're incompatible."

He threw his hands up. "Until five minutes ago, we were having a great time. Just because we disagree on one thing—"

"One major thing."

"You're making a simple issue too complicated." He frowned. "We're adults. We could manage to compromise."

Juliette doubted it. Compromise to him was probably a one-sided decision. No, thank you. Apparently, he was blind to her position on the issue. "It's a moot point, anyway. It's not like we're a couple or anything. Just write your article and be done with it."

"I'm not ready to be done with you."

His words reverberated inside her. She sucked in a breath as the waiter set their glasses of wine on the table. Juliette grabbed hers and gulped half of it down.

Mitch eased her glass away from her mouth. "Relax. I just want to get to know you better, not bite you."

She inhaled deeply, realizing she was handling this conversation with all the sophistication of a teenager on her first date. "Maybe not, but you're complicating matters."

"I'm not trying to complicate anything." He reached across the table, sliding her stiff fingers beneath his palm. "I'm just trying to find out how compatible we are. That's supposed to be our purpose here."

She affected a cool stare. "Well, since this is a business date, let's act like it, okay?"

"That would be great, except I think it's more than that. You know it, too. That's why you're so damn nervous."

He leaned back in his chair and crossed his arms over his wide chest. Juliette swallowed at the challenge in his gaze.

"What gave you that impression?"

"Honey, you can't run for long from the attraction between us. I've given up trying. Why won't you?"

The waiter approached, saving Juliette the difficulty of answering Mitch.

"Are you ready to order?" the tuxedo-clad man asked.

Mitch tossed a probing stare at her, heat roiling in his dark eyes. Her body temperature went up about twenty degrees. Even her palms started to sweat.

"Are you hungry?" he asked.

He wasn't talking about food. Judging from the waiter's tight smile, even he knew it.

She cleared her throat. "Lasagna, please. I'll have cauliflower as my vegetable and blue cheese on my salad."

He ordered linguini with red clam sauce and a salad with vinaigrette. As soon as the waiter bowed and departed, Juliette jumped up from her seat.

"I'm going to the rest room," she announced and fled, giving

Mitch no chance to comment.

In the ladies' room, the glare of yellow fluorescent lights and the odor of a strong floral air freshener did nothing to calm her nerves. Her stomach leapt as if it was practicing the high jump. Her heart raced like she was running a marathon. What on earth was wrong with her?

She leaned her head against the speckled gray granite beside the sink. How could one man and one day have her questioning her whole future? Okay, maybe she'd had a niggling of doubt before that marrying Andrew was not the best course for her future. But heck, only sheer willpower had kept her from forgetting Andrew altogether today. Illogically, she felt guilty that she didn't feel guilty for enjoying Mitch's company. That and the fact she could hardly sit still in her seat without wanting to attack Mitch every time the man tossed her one of those sexy, measuring stares.

Get yourself together. Act like a professional. Sticking her hands beneath a flow of cool water, Juliette took soothing breaths. She would not be baited or succumb to his teasing. He was a reporter; she a business owner. Her mission was to convince him to retract his first article's slant on A Perfect Match. That hardly added up to romance.

Juliette dried her hands and made her way to the table again, keeping those thoughts firmly in mind.

During the next few minutes, Mitch said little verbally, but spoke volumes with his eyes. He wanted her; he wasn't even attempting to hide it. He was going to do his best to seduce her. *Oh, God.*

She shifted in her chair, aware of a conspicuous ache in a very dangerous place.

When dinner arrived, it passed in a growing silence that connected more than separated them. She became aware of his breathing, watched the movements of his strong hands—wishing all the while she found him anything but fascinating.

Finally, the waiter arrived to take their plates away. "Would you care for dessert?"

They both declined, and Mitch asked for the check.

Thank God, this dream date with the timing from hell was about to end. Elation and relief should have filled her.

They didn't. She couldn't stop wondering what would happen next. If he would kiss her...and where she'd ever find the strength to resist.

The waiter handed Mitch the bill a few moments later. Straining to retain any amount of composure, Juliette stood as he handed the man some cash.

"Let's go." Mitch gestured toward the door, placing his other hand at the small of her back.

She shivered as they exited into the cool night air. Juliette told herself it was the temperature and not Mitch's touch that caused her to tremble.

Mitch helped her into the truck, then ran around to his side. As he started the vehicle, its engine roared, as if mimicking her revving heartbeat.

"Dinner was great," he commented. "Good choice of restaurants."

"Thanks."

Would he want to come in, have a drink? Her eyes slid shut. Or, dear Lord, would he try to kiss her good night? Press for more?

"In fact, I thought the whole day was great. This evening hasn't been bad so far, either."

Juliette nodded, her mind racing. Mitch's words seemed to intimate that the night wasn't over. She wasn't Catholic, but she felt the urge to cross herself and pray for extra restraint.

Twenty minutes later, Mitch turned his truck onto her street. Surely the emotion dragging her down was just exhaustion. After all, she couldn't feel any displeasure at this date ending and be any kind of a sane woman.

In that case, she probably needed a good psychiatrist.

When they pulled into the parking lot of her apartment complex, Mitch parked close to her place and cut the engine of his truck. "Let me walk you to your door."

She had to get away before he tried to kiss her...and she wasn't strong enough to resist.

"I'll be fine."

"I insist."

She opened her mouth to protest. He cut her off.

"Just two weeks ago, a woman in the Valley was killed for her ATM card after her jerk of a date dropped her off at the curb. I'm not risking that with you."

Put that way, Mitch's insistence made sense. Kara and Andrew both told her often that she trusted strangers too much.

"Okay. Thanks."

She climbed out of the truck and heard Mitch following suit. He followed her up the stairs to her front door, carrying her bag. Even without contact between them, his presence loomed strong, tickling her every nerve with awareness.

Dang it! Her horoscope this morning indicated it would be a great day for romance. She had hoped the astrologer was wrong.

Maybe she could still make a clean getaway. Juliette withdrew her key from her purse and opened her front door. Great. No lights on; no TV blaring. No Kara. She'd been hoping her little sister would play watchdog and ensure she kept her hands off Mitch. Instead, Kara had probably gone out with her girlfriends. She was on her own.

Stay cool, calm and professional, she reminded herself, drawing in a deep breath. Knowing that attitude would be easier to maintain outside her door than inside, she hovered in the threshold.

"Thanks for a lovely time." She held out her hand to him. "I enjoyed myself and hope you got lots of positive material for your next article."

He set her bag down and grasped her palm. His warmth seared her fingers. An electric tingle screamed along the length of her palm, up her arm.

"I had a great time, too," he said, his gaze riveted on her face.

He wanted to kiss her; his sultry dark stare said so with eloquent silence. All light-hearted replies fled Juliette's mind. Instead, she stood in her doorway, her hand clasped in Mitch's.

Wind whistled around them in a winter song. Juliette stared back at Mitch, watching the play of her porch light shadow his face. God, he was gorgeous...and kind, and fun, and smart.

He held her gaze in the snare of his own, and she couldn't find the will to look away.

"Juliette," he murmured. "Honey, don't look at me like that. It's taking every ounce of control I have right now to walk away."

His admission sent a fire zinging to her belly—and lower.

Mitch seemed smart. Was there any chance he was right, that she was blowing their differences of security and stability out of proportion?

Maybe, as he suggested, she shouldn't run from her true feelings, either. Living a lie would only cheat her, right? She would hate to look back at this missed opportunity and wonder what might have been. She had to know if her fantasies about Mitch had any reality.

"Kiss me," she whispered.

He sucked in a breath. "Are you sure?"

His question only made her more certain she had to know the truth, before giving Andrew her answer...before it was too late.

"We've got to prove or disprove that old wives' tale about first kisses, don't we? For your article, I mean." Juliette tried for flirty, but feared she sounded breathless and nervous.

At least that's how she felt.

Mitch didn't hesitate, didn't ask more questions. He just slid his hands up her arms, then cupped her face in his hands. He stared for a long moment, and Juliette sank into the dark lure of want burning in his gaze. The gong of her heartbeat flooded her ears and he leaned closer, closer.

His lips brushed her temple, her cheek, her jaw, so gently, like she was the most fragile thing he'd ever touched. Her insides were clawing for more, for his mouth on her own.

A moment later, his stare made his way back to hers. His fingers tightened at the back of her neck, holding her right under him.

Then his lips crashed over hers. Sensually. Perfectly. Juliette melted as his teeth nipped her lower lip. He tasted like passion, needy, possessive, as he urged her lips apart and sank deep, fondling her tongue with his own.

The sensation exploded a rush of desire in her belly. God, he kissed like he wanted her desperately, like he needed her more than his next breath. The way Juliette needed him.

She stood on her tiptoes and pressed against him...where she could have no doubts about how much he wanted her. She could feel his sizeable erection, especially when he caught her around the waist, then bent to fit himself right between her legs and pressed against her.

She gasped into his mouth, taking in his elemental masculine scent at the same time. Nothing she'd ever experienced had felt so untamed, so natural...so right.

If the old wives believed that first kisses proved something, this one proved Mitch had the ability to move the earth beneath her feet.

With a sigh, he lifted his head. Juliette heard his ragged breathing, which matched her own. The look in his eyes said he didn't want to quit.

Hungry for more, she didn't, couldn't, protest as he leaned close again. She tightened her arms about his neck and arched closer.

His mouth covered hers once more, fully, engulfing her in his taste and scent. Mitch's tongue penetrated the seam of her lips again, and she opened wider for him, dizzily reveling in their shared exhalations, the merciless caress of his mouth.

Heat surged through her blood, between her thighs. *Boom, boom*; her heart slammed against her ribs, drowning out what little logic she had left. Pressure and need zoomed low in her belly.

With the insistent press of his body, he backed her against the door, stroking his way over her curves with the skill of a master craftsman before burying his fingers in her hair. She moaned into his mouth, and he held her tighter. Drowning in the depth of her desire, in the pleasure of his solid form against hers, Juliette arched against him. It was an offering; nothing more, nothing less.

With Mitch, temptation and sin sounded like good words.

"So sweet," he panted against her lips. "Just like I imagined."

He'd imagined them kissing? Even though she had done the same, his admission infused her with a fresh thrill.

She reached up to press her lips to his again, opening beneath his demanding mouth. Want broiled between them when he stroked inside her, leaving his taste and a sting of desire behind. Mitch grabbed her tighter, pressed into her, their breaths mingling.

He kissed her hard, once, twice. His hand trailed off her shoulder and traced her collarbone before his thumb brushed the side of her breast. A trail of fire burned in his wake.

Then he broke away. "I have to stop now...or I won't."

Stop, yes. They had to; he was right. What they'd shared had been way more than a simple kiss. But a wild, impulsive part of her wanted to forget all the reason they shouldn't and think only about how fabulous sex would be between them.

Struggling to catch his breath, he laid his forehead against hers. "It's going to be impossible for me to walk away from you after today, after this kiss."

Ditto in double for her. Crazily enough, some part of her had become attached Mitch in the short time she'd known him. Could she walk away and ever marry Andrew? Ever settle down for stability when she knew excitement lay within reach, even if temporarily?

Frowning, she stepped out of his embrace. "I enjoyed myself. I'd forgotten being with someone could be such fun. Thank you."

He touched the side of her face, fingers brushing her jaw.

"Just remember that before you start planning your future."

Juliette couldn't forget his words for the next three days. Like a teenager, she stared at the phone on her desk, willing it to ring and jumping each time it did. Even more disconcerting, the sound of Andrew's voice on the other end of the line never failed to engender an initial stab of disappointment, followed by blade-twisting guilt. After all, if Mitch did call, she should simply tell him to write his article and never call again.

Instinctively, she knew that wouldn't solve her problem. Maybe Mitch was right. Perhaps she was running from the truth, from this burgeoning thing between them, and blowing their different concepts of a secure future out of proportion.

But she couldn't, wouldn't, live in dread again of the next imminent household move. She refused to leave behind friends and neighbors she never had the opportunity to meet. She would not put her children through the hell of changing schools every two months and condemn them—and herself—to lives of isolation.

Juliette lowered her head into her hands and sighed. Yet what kind of wife would she make to a man as deserving as Andrew if she had these feelings for Mitch? Refusing to admit her attraction to Mitch, would only feed his belief that her matchmaking methods were comprised of black magic and fairy dust.

"Phone call, line two," Connie, her receptionist, said over the intercom.

"Thanks." She grabbed the phone. "Hello?"

"Hi, Sis."

Juliette sighed in frustration. "What?"

"Don't sound so happy to talk to me," Kara said acidly.

"I'm sorry. I—I'm expecting a phone call." *Well, sort of.*

"You've been acting weird ever since your date with that reporter. So what happened that you're not telling me about? Hey, did you two get horizontal?"

Juliette winced. Kara had always known how to read her like a book. "No."

"Something happened. Have you seen this morning's *Signal*?" Kara asked, her voice laced with incredulity.

"Should I see it?"

"And how." Kara paused. "I don't know what you did, but you sure made an impression on that reporter."

Mitch's second article! "What do you mean?"

"Definitely different than the first article he wrote," Kara explained. "Oops. Gotta go," she whispered. "Boss is coming. Bye."

The line went dead. Different how? Good or bad?

Telling herself the butterflies in her stomach were not her nerves acting up, Juliette grabbed her purse and headed to The Brunchery. Inside, the last of the lunch crowd was dying down.

She bought a paper and a sandwich, then rushed back to her desk with both. Tossing the box containing her lunch on top of her printer, Juliette spread out the paper and began flipping through the pages. Finally, she found:

A Perfect Match in a Different Light, by Mitchell E. MacKinnon.

There was that word again, different. Meaning...?

Walk a mile in another's shoes, goes the old adage. After

questioning the validity of a local dating service, A Perfect Match, which employs methods such as a personality inventory and a dab of astrology, the service's owner, Juliette Lowell, challenged me to experience for myself the merits of her well-meaning business.

I issued her a counterchallenge, citing the fact she had never walked in her clients' shoes, either. She accepted, and the match-up was on.

I filled out an extensive online questionnaire, as does every client. To some, her questions might seem as difficult to grasp as a calculus textbook. Others might feel as though Ms. Lowell's forms were a cloaked but intense probing of the psyche. In either case, the respondent is asked approximately sixty questions, some more background gathering, others designed to peg temperament. This is followed by a request to define his or her description of the ideal mate. Ms. Lowell then conducts a bit of interviewing and inputs all information gathered into her database.

Ironically, Ms. Lowell herself turned out to be my "perfect match".

Because her literature suggests each party plan half of the first date as another means of judging compatibility, we agreed to do the same. I chose an afternoon of inline skating by the beach. Ms. Lowell selected an evening at the ballet. Neither of us seemed overly excited about the activity the other had planned.

Skeptics might say that such a disparity in choices of leisure pursuits points to anything but a "perfect match". Optimists might argue, however, that one date is hardly enough time to judge the possibility of lifelong compatibility.

Since I tend to be something of an optimist, I'm going to agree with that theory, partially because Ms. Lowell and I had a highly pleasant date, despite engaging in activities foreign to us.

And if we accept the optimists' hypothesis that one date isn't enough to judge much of anything, we can ask but one question if we truly want to discern the merits of Ms. Lowell's business:

How about a second date?

A second date? Her heart soared. Adrenaline curled through her limbs. Anticipation and anxiety warred for her brain.

No. Positively not. She couldn't go, not if she wanted to avoid sinking any deeper into the abyss of her attraction to the meandering Mitch.

She and Mitch had clicked. She could not deny that. But if she accepted Mitch's invitation, she feared she'd be jeopardizing a stable future with Andrew. Worse, if she listened to her intuition and attempted to forge a relationship with Mitch, she might end up sacrificing what *she* needed and wanted to stay with her man, as her mother had done.

She vowed to be smarter than that.

But what about passion? Andrew, admittedly, didn't thrill her. Mitch definitely did. They connected on multiple levels, physical, emotional, intellectual. That kind of link didn't happen every day.

What a mess! Either she sacrificed the stability she'd always wanted for an exciting man who might well pack up and move on next week, or she lived the rest of her days with a man who couldn't raise her pulse as quickly as a brisk walk.

Where was the answer in that?

In Milwaukee, she decided. One phone call to Wisconsin could prove her wrong. After all, it was easy to lose the bond with someone twenty-five hundred miles away, and much simpler to hone in on your connection to someone in your own backyard.

Certainly, a brief conversation with Andrew would prove she shared some sort of chemistry with him that she'd simply forgotten.

Juliette reached for the phone and dialed the number of Andrew's hotel. Surprisingly enough, he answered.

"Yes?" came his deep voice.

"Hi. Do you have a minute?"

"Sure, darling," Andrew greeted. "How is your day?"

She swallowed. What could she say to Andrew about her feelings for Mitch? "It's all right. And yours?"

There was a shrug in his voice. "As well as a day in the boardroom ever goes. All these meetings are so long."

To her dismay, she found herself missing their friendship far more than their romantic connection. She had over the past few days, however, completely missed talking to Mitch, laughing at his jokes, watching the play of his dimples, tasting the hot demand of his kiss.

"You'll be home in a couple of weeks," she said.

"And you'll have an answer for me then, won't you, pumpkin?"

Pumpkin? "I promised I would."

"Anything you want to tell me now?"

Juliette paused. The only words that sprang to mind were an admission of her confusing feelings for Mitch. To make matters worse, she didn't feel even the smallest tingle at hearing Andrew's voice.

"Actually, I ah...called to tell you about the second article in *The Signal*," she finally blurted.

"About A Perfect Match? Mom read it to me earlier."

"Well, what do you think?"

"I don't love the idea of you seeing him again. After all, you're almost mine."

Though she understood his perspective, the way Andrew put it irked her. She wasn't a puppy he could register with the A.K.C.

"But," Andrew continued, "I can understand the man's point."

Gritting her teeth together, she replied, "It's true he has the power to say some really positive things about my business. I know it could make a positive impact."

"Which is why I think you should go."

Seriously? "Isn't it difficult to think of me with another man while you're so far away?"

"I trust you. Besides, there's no telling what the man will write if you say no." His reasoning was logical, even valid.

But Andrew was only helping her rationalize reasons she should go out with another man. Which was exactly what she wanted to do. Juliette itched to spend more time with Mitch, explore the baffling emotions he made her feel, even if doing so was as smart as playing in traffic.

She knew erasing Mitch from her life and thoughts would be the smartest course of action. Unfortunately, she'd never been considered an honor student.

"I know..."

"You could play it safe, if you want. You don't owe MacKinnon a damn thing. But why tell him that another date would be impossible? If you go now, this little mess might be resolved before I get home. Then you can focus on us. Besides, it's not as if you two are planning an actual romantic evening."

If Mitch had his way... "Well, actually, I think that's exactly what he's planning."

"Focus on business. He's offering you free advertising."

"But I'd still be dating a man who's a little...overwhelming."

"Look, some transient former jock who's become a two-bit reporter will never seriously catch your attention. What you and I have is too solid and stable, is based on mutual respect and a shared vision of the future. A follow-up date for business purposes with this guy isn't going to change that."

Before she'd been on a date with Mitch, she would have agreed wholeheartedly. Now...

"I think you should go," Andrew went on. "The consequences if you turn this date down could be too high. Besides, I want you to know that I support you and A Perfect Match completely. Besides, it doesn't look as though this reporter has given you a choice."

That, Juliette agreed with. Andrew supported her. *Fabulous.* Logic told her that should make her happy. Instead she felt miserably confused. She should want Andrew's support, but his lack of jealousy and his overconfidence in his position in her life annoyed her. He was acting as if he already had the ring on her finger.

Chapter Seven

Mitch glanced at his watch. Two p.m. Had Juliette seen the article? Read it? Loved or hated it? Why hadn't she called to respond? He picked up his phone and started to dial Juliette's number, then set the receiver down once more.

"She'll call," Dave muttered from the desk beside him. "With an invitation like the one you left dangling in that article, she'll call."

Mitch sighed. "I wish I were as convinced as you. She's skittish. Almost engaged to someone else. I should be a nice guy and just leave her alone. But I can't."

"You like this girl. If she isn't engaged or married yet, she's fair game."

His sentiments exactly.

What if Juliette had retreated again, certain they couldn't work their differences out? He hoped not, not when this something between them felt like more than passing attraction. More like a firebomb of good chemistry. Now that his series of articles about her business was most likely over, he'd have an opportunity to persuade her of that truth without business getting in the way.

The phone rang. He all but jumped on the receiver. "MacKinnon." *Please let it be Juliette.*

"Mitch, my boy. I want to see you."

His shoulders sagged at the sound of his editor's voice. "John, can it wait a few minutes? I'm expecting a phone call."

"We have voicemail. You can call whoever back later. This is hot."

He held in a groan. "I'll be right there."

With a long sigh, Mitch replaced the phone in its cradle and trudged to John's office.

"Yeah?" he said, poking his head in the door.

John frowned. "With that face, you could make the grim reaper look as funny as a stand-up comic. Sit down."

Mitch made his way through the maze of John's cluttered office and folded himself into the hard chair. "What's up?"

"Your article about A Perfect Match. My Louise loved it, and this phone has been ringing off the hook all day long! My inbox has exploded."

"Great," Mitch said less than enthusiastically. If everyone loved it so much, why hadn't Juliette called?

"Circulation is really up today. People are saying this is better than *As the World Turns.*"

Yippie Skippy. Now the citizens of Santa Clarita thought his life was as dramatic as a soap opera. Would Juliette, in true serial drama form, marry Andrew then discover too late that she'd made a mistake?

"Isn't that great?" John prompted.

"Fab."

"Even Russ Kendrick heard about the increase in circulation and called to ask what all the hoopla was about."

Mitch's ears finally perked up. "He did?"

John nodded his graying head. "So I faxed him copies of

your articles about A Perfect Match. I also mentioned what a great sports writer you are. He remembered when you used to play for University of Miami."

The editor-in-chief of *USA Today* had inquired about him, had copies of his articles in hand? Definitely something to get excited about. It wouldn't solve his dilemma about Juliette, but if he played his cards right, he might move onto something big.

"Did he say anything else?" Mitch prodded.

"He asked for your phone number. I gave it to him."

His boss and friend had just handed him his best opportunity at the big time, as promised. "Do you think I should take a proactive stance to call Russ Kendrick? I have other samples of work I'd love to show him."

"Absolutely," John answered. "Russ likes aggressive reporters."

Mitch thrust his hand toward John. "Thanks. A lot. You've given me a great opportunity."

The other man shook his hand. "No, I gave you the exposure. Your insight and words are creating the opportunity for you. Good luck." He released Mitch's hand and gestured to the door. "Now get out of here. I've got a paper to run, and you've got a date to make."

Juliette. If he got the job with Kendrick, he'd almost certainly have to move. With an ordinary woman, he'd simply give her up and move onto the next. Walking away from Juliette wasn't something he wanted to do. He needed to test the attraction between them. But if he stepped one toe out of Santa Clarita, he suspected she'd label him overly reckless and write him out of her life as too big of a risk.

Wandering back to his desk, Mitch sighed. This was crazy. Juliette Lowell was making him crazy. Why was he sitting here wondering how she would feel if he moved? They'd had one date, which he'd had to coerce out of her. She was seeing another man, almost engaged to him. None of that added up to any real relationship potential. He hadn't pictured a wife, or even a steady girlfriend, at this point in his life. Yet here he was thinking about Juliette in serious terms.

Maybe he needed sleep, to see a shrink or get laid. He plopped down into his desk chair. No, what he needed was to see Juliette again, really spend some time with her so he could figure out what was between them.

He had to. Right now, he felt certain that moving away without exploring the chemistry between them would be synonymous with sacrificing one opportunity for another.

Mitch returned to his desk to find a blinking light on his phone. A voicemail. He punched his code and listened to Juliette haltingly ask him to call her back.

"Oh, God," Mitch muttered to himself.

"Juliette?" At Mitch's nod, Dave laughed beside him. "I hate to say I told you so, but..."

"I don't know her answer yet, so can it."

He grabbed the phone and dialed Juliette's number. Connie put him right through.

"Hello?" Juliette answered. Her voice trembled.

He had to proceed carefully. He feared she would run fast if he didn't. "Thanks for calling. I assume you've read the article?"

"Yes. Thank you for your...optimism."

"I tried to be fair." Tension knotted his stomach. He grabbed a pencil and thrummed its eraser against his desk. "Are you going to answer the question I posed in the article?"

"Yes."

Mitch tossed aside the pencil and sat up straighter. "Yes, you have an answer, or yes, you'll go out with me again?"

The silence emanating from her end of the line had Mitch curling his hands into fists. God, why did he want her to say yes on both counts so badly?

"Yes, I'll go out with you again," she finally said.

Mitch released the breath he'd been holding and leaned back in his chair. Relief burst in his system with the strength of a sonic boom. "When?"

He heard her flip through the pages of her calendar. "I've got a fundraiser to attend Saturday afternoon." She exhaled raggedly. "And I'm supposed to go to a Christmas party with my sister that night. Are you free Sunday?"

He swore under his breath. "Sunday afternoon I'm scheduled to cover the Chargers' game in San Diego for the paper. I've got to be at the stadium by noon. That night, I promised to take my mother out to dinner for her birthday. What about next weekend?"

She paused. "That's Christmas weekend. I'll be all tied up. How does this Friday night look for you?"

"I'm supposed to cover Valencia High's playoff game. But I'd love to have you come along, if you don't hate football too much."

"I've never really watched it," she confessed. "Maybe you'll teach me to like it." Her laugh carried a nervous echo.

Mitch frowned. "Are you all right?"

"Fine."

Her quick, monosyllabic answer sounded anything but. In fact, she sounded almost resigned. Whatever bothered her, she clearly didn't want to discuss it with him. After all, they'd had only one date. He shouldn't expect her to pour her heart out to him. But it rankled him that she wouldn't share her troubles.

Since when have you ever wanted a woman pouring out her

troubles to you? Since now...

"Can I pick you up at six-thirty?" he asked, consciously softening his tone. "The game starts at eight."

"Fine."

He gnashed his teeth together, wishing she'd say something besides fine. But if he kept pushing her to say what was on her mind, he had this feeling she'd only clam up more.

"See you then," he finally settled for, then hung up.

He couldn't help but wonder if Friday night would bring victory or defeat, and not for the home football team.

For him and Juliette.

Friday's twilight faded into a clear, midnight blue evening, punctuated by crystal stars and a Santa Ana wind. A night for romance, despite their jeans and sweatshirts.

She and Mitch munched on hot dogs and sipped cocoa in the press box at the junior college where the local high school games were held, waiting for the game to begin.

Absently, Juliette watched the two teams running through warm-up exercises on the muddy field. Anything to take her eyes off Mitch. As usual, his faded denim jeans hugged his muscled thighs and butt so nicely, she could hardly string two intelligent words together. Why did she want to touch him, even knowing Mitch could never give her the kind of future she needed?

Behind her, other reporters and a coach or two gathered in the same small room. A balding man flipped switches in front of her, testing lights and the scoreboard. A nervous pacer in the corner cursed under his breath.

She had to get out of here, talk to Mitch alone. She needed

to sort out her thoughts and understand what was happening to her emotionally. Her stomach felt like a ticking time bomb with less than a minute before detonation.

Mitch touched her shoulder. Juliette started, gasping at the tingling burn his touch ignited.

"I didn't mean to startle you," he said, his brow wrinkling in confusion. "You okay?"

"Fine."

Juliette felt like a parrot with a one-word vocabulary. She knew Mitch wanted to hear more than that one false syllable. At that moment, especially in the press box, she didn't know what else to say.

"We've got half an hour before the game starts," he added. "I interviewed all the key players earlier in the evening, so I can take a short break. How about a walk?"

Either he'd read her mind or harbored similar feelings. Nodding, Juliette headed for the door. Mitch followed.

In the cool evening breeze, Mitch took her hand and led her down the metal stairs, to the ground level behind the bleachers. As they veered away from the concession stand, his hand around hers seemed to reach inside, to her heart, and squeeze.

She wished Andrew's touch would affect her this way.

They paused beneath a tree, its bare branches whipping in the wind above them. Mitch leaned against its scarred trunk with a sigh. "You've been awfully quiet since I picked you up. You were quiet the last time I talked to you. Wanna tell me what's wrong?"

She had no idea where to start or how much to say. Andrew had all but pushed her into this date. Testing this "thing" between them once and for all to see if she could rid herself of these feelings for Mitch should be her goal. Now the idea terrified her.

"It's us, isn't it? You're scared," he prompted.

She nodded. "It's silly..."

"If you're scared, it's not." He cocked his head to one side, apparently in thought. "What did you think of our first date, Juliette?"

"I had a great time." She spoke slowly, softly. "I told you that."

"How did you come away feeling? Like you just had a pleasant time or..." he paused, leaning closer, "...that there could be something...more?"

He eased his arm around her shoulders. Wanting his touch, knowing she shouldn't, Juliette tensed.

"If 'more' means sexually, I don't have meaningless flings. I just can't have sex with men I don't care about."

He stroked her cheek with the pad of his thumb. "First, I'm beginning to really suspect that what we could have is anything but meaningless. Second, when I said 'something more,' I wasn't talking just about your body, although that would be nice to have."

The corners of his mouth lifted, and Juliette felt the impact of that smile all through her.

"I want to be with you, because it's you," he continued. "I can't explain it, but more than my libido is involved."

Juliette's heart began to pound. "Oh."

Mitch's thumb traced the slope of her neck. "What do you think we have between us?"

Wow, this conversation had to set a world record for getting to the point. "I don't know. That's partially why I agreed to this date."

"We're at the same place, then," Mitch said, bringing her

closer, his face buried in her hair.

Now what? Pull away, or explore further, until she knew if saying yes to Andrew was right—or dead wrong. She swallowed as he brought her face under his and looked directly into her eyes.

"You look terrified," he said, his tone almost joking.

She raised her gaze to his face. "I'm not terribly comfortable, since we have different concepts of the future. Remember?"

"Not completely. I think we could talk it out."

"We've only known each other a short time."

"Exactly. Maybe our views aren't as different as they seem. We got along great with everything else we did."

The memory of his mouth on hers flashed through her mind. "Maybe too well." She paused. "What happened at the end of our last date shouldn't have happened. Our evening together was supposed to be business, and that kiss... It wasn't fair to Andrew. And it only confused the issue."

"I assume you asked me to kiss you because that's what you wanted."

She bit her lip. Her throat tightened with emotion. "I...guess I wanted to know if what I felt was real and mutual."

Mitch reached for her hand and rubbed his thumb over its bare third finger. "Do you love Brimmley? Honestly?"

Her eyes slid shut. Her answer wasn't a simple yes or no; Mitch had to know that. Turning away, she wondered how one small question could rattle her with such conflicting emotions.

"What's not to love about him?" she finally said, opening her eyes. "He's intelligent, and...and caring—"

"That's not what I asked. Do you *love* him?"

Juliette tilted her head back, staring blindly into the barren tree branches above. The spindly appendages looked forlorn. Funny, she'd never thought her life would mimic a tree. Apparently, there was a first for everything.

Sighing, she searched deep in places she didn't want to. This was the answer she'd come to find. Running from it now might ruin her whole future.

Finally, she said, "I love a lot of things about him. He's kind. He'll make a great father, a caring husband—"

"But you're not *in* love with him."

There it was, the naked truth. Juliette wished she were curled up in her bed with the Raggedy Ann doll her mother had given her for her eighth birthday. Away from Mitch's distracting influence, she'd have a better chance of sorting out her life. His piercing gaze demanded a response now.

"Maybe it will grow in time," she said. "I care for him. He'll give me the stability I want."

Silence followed her answer. Mitch dropped his hand from her hair and leaned in, his face and body inches away. Again, that pang, that need he ignited in her, flared with new life. Damn him.

"Stability?" Mitch repeated. Juliette had a hard time concentrating as his dark gaze slid across her face, melted into her eyes. "What comfort will that be when you're married to a man who can't do this for you?"

Mitch whirled her, pinning her to the tree trunk. Their bodies touched at thigh, at hip. The hard heat of his chest connected with hers as their mouths met. Juliette's resistance buckled under the persuasive pressure of Mitch's kiss. Her heart slammed into her chest. Her sex went up in flames the instant he touched her.

She held him tightly, a haze of desire drumming through her body. His tongue penetrated her mouth, probing deeply, demanding her response. Desire, like ooey-gooey honey, oozed all through her. Juliette found it impossible not to kiss him back, not to return the insistent strokes of his tongue, so coaxing she could have cried.

He caressed her back, stroked her shoulder—and pressed his full length against her, putting her between a hard place and a proverbial rock. And she clung to him, trying to devour his mouth, gripping his biceps, smoothing her palms across his pecs, clutching at his back as he took the kiss deeper...deeper.

God, she wished Andrew could make her feel a tenth of this desire. Her life would be so much simpler.

Mitch leaned away, bracing his arm against the tree trunk above her. "That's not simple lust. I know it. I think you know it, too." He paused, breathing hard. "What are we going to do about it?"

She shook her head. Mitch and his kisses were trying to alter her future with the speed of a Learjet. "I don't know. Who says we have to *do* something?"

He traced her bottom lip with his thumb. She shivered.

"We've taken the time to figure this much out, and you—"

"Andrew may not ignite me," she broke in, suddenly angry. "But at least he won't come home one afternoon and tell me I have three days to pack up the house, gather the children and traipse across country for the sake of his job."

"If you don't feel with him what we just shared, you might not have those kids or care if he wants to leave," he pointed out. "Besides, what makes you think I would do that?"

Juliette gaped at him in incredulity. "You're moving away just as soon as a better job comes along. You said so yourself. You treat moving like it's an adventure."

Mitch grabbed her shoulders and pulled her closer. "I have

no one to worry about but me. If I had a wife and children…" he shook his head, "…that would be different. Yeah, there might be some moves, but they'd be carefully planned by both of us."

She stepped back, retreating from his proximity. "I want to live in one house, raise my children there, see them through that school district, know the members of the community, have them know me—"

"That's important enough to make you marry the wrong man?"

Juliette swallowed a quick *yes*. She stared at Mitch, gazed into his eyes, his soul. Somehow, she knew if she said that stability was crucial enough to marry Andrew, she'd never see Mitch again.

She put her face in her hands. What good was stability if every other part of her life made her unhappy?

As if sensing her turmoil, Mitch enveloped her in his arms. His palms soothed her back. She melted against him like butter in the microwave.

"Look, I'm not sure how to say this, but I've come to…feel something for you, as corny as that sounds. And you don't seem indifferent to me." He sighed. "I think we owe it to ourselves to discover what's really there."

Maybe Mitch was right. If she was destined to have these feelings for him, wasn't she smarter to discover it now? She had to figure out once and for all which was more important, security or excitement. In her case, the two appeared mutually exclusive.

She nodded. "I'll think about it."

He stroked her hair and kissed her forehead. "Come on. The game's about to start. Want another cup of cocoa?"

She smiled, despite her confusion. "I never refuse

chocolate."

With a nod, Mitch took her hand, and led her toward the concession stand. They stood in line, under the lights. Darkness reigned behind them. The breeze kicked up her hair. She hugged herself, hoping she could make the right decision—before Andrew returned from Milwaukee and demanded an answer.

From the front of the line, she spotted a familiar face. One of her clients turned with his hands full of snacks. Juliette smiled.

The man's eyes narrowed.

Reflexively, she backed away at his fury. "Joe? What's wrong? Are you okay?"

"No, I'm not," he snarled. "I tried to call you last week, but your snotty receptionist said you were gone."

"I'm sorry. She didn't leave me a message or I would have called—"

"I told her not to leave one," he bit out.

"Why? What's—"

"Wrong?" Joe interrupted. "My date, my 'perfect match', ended up being an efficient little thief. We went back to my place for coffee after a movie. I woke up with a splitting headache and everything of value in my house was gone, including my credit cards, which she used all night long."

Juliette gasped. "Oh, Joe... I'm shocked. I..." She grappled for words, staring at her client in blinking incomprehension. "I don't know what to say. Rita seemed like such a sweet girl—"

"I called the cops and found out she's wanted in two other states."

Juliette paused as the shock settled in. This was her worst nightmare; that someone not committed to finding their perfect match would make it past her screening and exploit all her lonely clients.

"I'm so sorry. I'll refund all your fees and file a claim with my insurance company. If you can think of anything else—"

"I've already filed with my insurance company."

His anger triggered a shot of guilt. After all, Joe was paying the price for her carelessness. "I... Tell me how I can make amends."

"You can't." He shook his head. "But I'm going to make sure no one else suffers what I have."

With that threat, Joe stalked off.

Juliette's shoulders sagged, her mind racing. The press? *The Signal*?

With questioning eyes, she turned to Mitch.

He gave his attention to the woman behind the counter, as if he hadn't heard the whole encounter. "Two hot cocoas, please."

Juliette watched anxiously as Mitch handed the older woman money and waited in stiff silence for his change. A moment later, she handed him two steaming Styrofoam cups. He took them and turned away.

"Mitch?" Juliette heard the desperate note in her own voice.

God, she stood to lose everything— Andrew, if he discovered her true feelings, as well as her hard-earned success, if Mitch printed Joe's story in *The Signal*.

"Let's not talk about it now. We're here for the game and a chance to get to know each other better. Let's leave this story back at the office."

Did that mean he wouldn't take this story to the office with him? No, his ethics wouldn't allow that. They shouldn't. But the reluctance on his face told her that he wasn't eager to rush into this story, not like he would have been before their first date. That had to count for something, right? Maybe that meant he'd be gentle because he was beginning to believe...

Juliette exhaled nervously, hoping that was the case. She wanted to trust Mitch with her business reputation—and her heart—so badly it scared her.

☙

Deprived of sleep last night for thinking about Juliette, Mitch watched Dave stride in the following Monday. His co-worker wore a cocky grin that grated on Mitch's considerable grouchiness. Dave approached his desk with a swagger, then set his briefcase down with a sigh reminiscent of pure pleasure.

"Did you eat a canary or something?" Mitch snapped.

Dave just smiled wider and flipped open the black lid of his briefcase. He withdrew a catalog and, with a flick of his wrist, sent it flying into Mitch's desk. "Or something."

Mitch glanced down at the glossy photos. A picture of a tall, tanned model in nothing more than a black teddy, thigh high hose and tongue-swallowing stilettos greeted his gaze.

"You got Callie to wear this?" Amazement laced Mitch's voice.

He couldn't even recall the last time a woman had done her Victoria's Secret impression for him. But he knew immediately who he'd like the next someone to be. No doubt, he'd remember it too—even if he became ninety and senile. Just the thought of Juliette dressed up in such an outfit was enough to make his slacks a bit uncomfortable. But it wasn't likely to happen with their relationship in its present state. Why hadn't she called?

"Amen, brother. I call that my weekend getaway special,"

Dave added. At Mitch's surprised expression, he continued, "Marriage has a way of making a man happy. You single guys are just too caught up in the jungle to see it."

"At least we're free to roam," Mitch quipped.

Dave sent his a withering glance. "Callie hardly keeps me in a cage."

"True, but as a single guy, you can just pick up and go anywhere with anyone, for whatever reason. No one to check with, no one to worry about. No problems."

"After I met Callie, that just wasn't fun anymore."

Mitch stared at his friend. The whole concept of not missing the freedom to go and do as he pleased seemed so twisted, Mitch could hardly fathom it. But Dave looked completely serious and relaxed. And hadn't he read a statistic that married men tended to live longer, happier lives?

"What about weekends with the guys?" he asked. "Heck, what about your career? Don't you ever worry you're missing out on life because you're stuck here?"

Dave laughed. "You sound just like me five years ago. I couldn't understand why anyone would work for a little paper like *The Signal* when better opportunities existed. I dreamed of assignments in Moscow and Paris, even the South Pole. I loved to travel. Every day was a new adventure."

"Yeah," Mitch seconded with a frown. "And you don't miss that?"

"Nah. I mean I still enjoy traveling. And I wouldn't be human if I didn't have a twinge every once in a while when I hear about a colleague who's hit the big time. But my adventure in life now is about my relationship, not my suitcase."

Mitch shook his head in confusion. "How is a relationship an adventure?"

Dave shrugged. "You know shit about love, man."

"Never been in it."

The smile on Dave's face looked close to gloating. "When you love someone, your excitement in life is more about who you're with than where you go," he explained. "If I was offered a story in Kenya tomorrow, I'd likely go for my career, but I'd miss Callie too much to think of it as serious fun. That's what happens when you've found who you're looking for."

Mitch contemplated Dave's words. He'd missed Juliette lately, true enough. Last night, while huddled around a smoky table playing poker for matchsticks with his single buddies, he'd been wondering what Juliette was doing. A part of him had even wanted to be with her instead of staring at dog-eared cards. Maybe that feeling was similar to what Dave had described.

Did that mean he loved Juliette? Mitch paused. He more than just liked her. In fact, she consumed more of his brain waves every day. He looked forward to seeing her whenever he could, whether they fought or not.

Love. Wow. It was possible, he supposed.

"How long have you been married now?" Mitch asked.

"Four years next month."

"And you're really happy?"

"Absolutely. I mean it's not perfect all the time. We fight like everyone else. But we make up, so that's fun." He laughed. "The rest of the time, we just get along. She really is my best friend."

"You don't mind living the rest of your life in Santa Clarita?"

Dave shrugged. "I like it here because I'm with her. That's most important to me now."

"You really don't miss the adventure of new places?"

"You're not listening. It doesn't matter where you are, just who you're with. Besides, after we have kids and they get a little older, we'll travel together, which will be ten times better than going alone. And until then," he grinned, "we find other ways to create adventures of our own."

Mitch was still pondering Dave's words his phone rang. Joseph Tarton—the same Joe who had accosted Juliette at the football game. Though he'd already heard the man's basic story, Mitch listened again.

A sinking feeling permeated his every cell as the man retold his tale. Theft was a real story. Any *Signal* reader contemplating joining A Perfect Match, or any other dating service, had a right to know that what happened to Joe Tarton could happen to them.

But he didn't want to be the one to write the article.

He'd made such strides with Juliette Friday night, convinced her to admit she felt something for him that she didn't feel for Brimmley. Reporting Mr. Tarton's story to the public would ensure Juliette's departure from his life at a time he wasn't sure he wanted to let her go.

But shelving this story for the sake of his personal life went against every ethic he believed. Turning a deaf ear was the one action he had no business taking if he wanted to write for Russ Kendrick and *USA Today*.

A moment later, his editor strolled by his desk.

"John," he called out.

His boss turned. "Hi, Mitch. What's up?"

Mitch gripped his pen between white fingers. "Is there any

way you could reassign the Perfect Match thing to someone else? I've got a new scoop, but I'm too close to it. Too involved to be effective anymore."

John clapped him on the back. "That's when you have to dig deep. Find out what kind of reporter you are and prove it to the world."

"But—"

"You'll do fine. Just put aside your personal feelings and plunge into the story."

With that bit of wisdom, John walked away.

Just fucking perfect. Cursing, Mitch turned to his computer.

ᴄᴙ

As of Tuesday afternoon, Juliette hadn't heard from Mitch since their Friday night date. At least four dozen times a day, she thought about calling him, only to set the phone back in its cradle, undialed.

She wondered if Mitch thought about her and wanted her answer about any kind of relationship between them, which she didn't have. What if he'd been writing Joe's story, anticipating his departure from *The Signal*, Santa Clarita and her life?

No, she had to believe that Mitch wouldn't completely stab her in the back now that they were getting closer, exploring the feelings between them. But he was very committed to his work, even more than she was to hers. And she couldn't ask him not to do his job.

She shook her head, hoping her good sense would return after three restless nights of circular logic and longings for the heat and promise of Mitch's touch.

And unfortunately, Joe Tarton hadn't cooled down any.

She'd tried to call him to offer apologies and reparations several times in the last few days. Each time, he'd hung up.

The phone rang, interrupting her reverie. She ran from the fax machine down the hall to her office, all but spilling her soda to answer breathlessly, "Hello?"

"Juliette. It's Mitch."

The voice she'd been desperate yet afraid to hear since Saturday morning. Her heart revved into a pounding pace.

"Hi," she greeted back.

"I need to see you tonight, just for a few minutes. Can you see me?"

The gravity in his tone told her he wanted to talk. Maybe he wanted her decision on their relationship...or about Joe's story. She leaned her forehead against her computer screen and sighed. Snap decisions had never been her forte, at least not good ones. As for decisions that affected the rest of her life. She never knew whether to follow her heart or listen to her head.

She frowned. "Is everything all right?"

"If it's okay, I can drop by your place tonight? I'll only stay a minute," he answered cryptically.

Foreboding flooded her stomach. He only wanted to stay a minute. Not a good sign. Maybe he'd decided they weren't meant for each other after all. That announcement would certainly take the complication out of life.

In that instant, she also knew it would leave her heartbroken. *Oh, God.*

"Okay," she finally answered. "Come about six. I can make dinner, if you want to stay."

"I wasn't asking for an invitation."

"Well, you've got one," she said, hoping to lighten his mood.

"I just need to talk to you."

Again, that urgency in his voice. She gripped the phone tighter. "What about? Is something wrong, Mitch?"

"We'll talk tonight. I promise," he said, then hung up.

What did he want? Maybe he planned to tell to take a long walk on a short bridge. She had no way of knowing, but the latter stabbed her with pain dangerously near her heart.

Was she in love with Mitch?

With slumped shoulders, she leaned away from her computer. She wished Mitch was easy to read, like Andrew. But no, he had to be complex, exciting, fascinating. All that and gorgeous. His dimples didn't help her decision any, either.

Juliette glanced at the digital clock on her desk, chewing on the ragged edge of a fingernail. Three red numbers glared out two-o-six in the afternoon.

Four hours and counting. Four hours of wondering what Mr. MacKinnon had up his sleeve—or in his heart.

Chapter Eight

Juliette scurried around her kitchen, lifting the lid on the simmering green beans and checking the chicken in the oven. She glanced at the clock on the stove; 5:56. Four more minutes, then Mitch would explain the strange tone of his phone call. Her curiosity was worse than the stuff that killed the cat.

The foreboding in her gut told her this was the equivalent of a "Dear Jane" meeting. And despite the fact Mitch wasn't—and never had been—hers, she was already mourning his loss from her life.

She'd seen no sign of Kara. Not that she was ever home much before eight, but Juliette had hoped her sister might be around, just in case things heated up between her and Mitch. Wishful thinking. Now, she'd have to rely on her own self-control. Scary.

Tearing off her apron, she ran for the bathroom and fussed with her hair. She shook like a teenager before her prom. Whatever happened to restraint and propriety? Applying a fresh coat of lipstick, she decided those two virtues had probably gone out with hoop skirts.

A knock sounded at the door. She took a deep breath, flipped off the light in the bathroom and hurried across her apartment.

She opened the door. Mitch stood in its frame, filling the

portal with his wide, athletic shoulders encased in a tight black athletic shirt with long sleeves that accentuated bulging biceps. His faded jeans hugged all the right places, lovingly cupping parts of him she'd recently been fantasizing about. As always, though, it was his eyes—dark, direct, penetrating. She sizzled from just his stare and sucked in a breath, trying to calm her dancing nerves.

"Hi," she said, pulling the door further open. "What's wrong? You look like you've lost your best friend."

"Not exactly, but I might lose someone I'd like to keep." He clasped her hand in his. "You."

Juliette closed the door behind him and followed him into the living room. Her stomach knotted. He wanted to keep her? The relief that flooded her after those words scared the hell out of her.

"If this is about our discussion last Friday night, I haven't made a decision. I—"

"That's not what I mean, at least not specifically." Mitch followed her across the room.

"What then?"

Mitch sighed and sat on the edge of her sofa. When he looked up at her, dark circles surrounded his chocolate eyes and his dimples were nowhere to be seen. "I just don't want to lose whatever chance I have with you."

Juliette sat beside him and restrained an urge to touch him. "Why do you think you would?"

"I wrote another article." He sighed. "About Joe Tarton's experience." He hung his head and twisted his watch on his wrist. "The article will run the day after Christmas."

The buzzer timing her chicken sounded from the kitchen as anxiety infused her system. Juliette didn't move. The timer droned on as Mitch's words seeped into her consciousness.

"I see." The buzzer nearly drowned out her slow whisper. "I'd hoped that after Friday night—"

"This has nothing to do with us, I swear. Hell, I even tried to have the story reassigned." He stood and strode to the kitchen and silenced the buzzer. "But I can't not do my job."

She frowned. "I know. And I wouldn't ask you to lie. But I hope you balanced his experience with all the other happy ones."

Mitch didn't say a word.

Foreboding brewed in her gut. "I thought you were beginning to understand my business, to believe in me."

"What happened to Joe could happen to anyone involved with any dating service," he argued. "I went out of my way to avoid pointing a finger at you and your business and state this is a potential pitfall of being single and looking."

Juliette watched Mitch rake tense hands through his hair. Her first urge was to run to the kitchen and comfort him. She resisted.

"So what did you write?" she asked instead, careful to keep her voice modulated and calm.

"Nothing more than I had to. I wrote as benignly as possible. I even got a quote from a deputy sheriff stating that this kind of thing almost never happens." He strode from the kitchen back to the living room. "I wanted to tell you first."

Logic told her he hadn't written his latest article to undermine or defame her. Reporting facts was his job; she knew that. He had even made special arrangements to tell her in person before the article hit the newsstands. And from everything he'd said, he had even tried to neutralize what could have been the most damaging piece of news about her business ever.

He would only do those things because he cared about her. He'd said he didn't want to lose her, so this connection they shared meant *something* to him. It was probably stupid, but the possibility warmed her all over.

Mitch walked to the door and heaved a heavy sigh. "I'm sorry. I'll...go now."

She rushed after him. "Wait. I...I know you didn't have to come here and tell me about the article. Thanks for your honesty."

He nodded but made no comment as he reached for the doorknob.

"I appreciate the fact you tried to soften this news in presenting it to the community. It could have been pretty harmful if you hadn't."

Mitch turned back to her and touched her cheek. "Just us, off the record? I wish like hell I could have gotten out of this article. The last thing I want to do is upset you, baby."

Baby. The depth of his sincerity seemed to shimmer from his deep brown eyes. Her heart was doing the Riverdance in her chest as she smiled and stepped toward him. "Thank you. Do you have to rush off? I made dinner."

He grasped her hand and drew her closer. "I could be persuaded to stay for a while."

Their eyes met. His gaze pulled her in. The air between them turned heavy.

Juliette knew what was coming, but could no more make herself step away than part the Red Sea. Mitch wrapped his palm around her nape and pulled her face toward his. For a split second, he paused. Juliette watched hunger and longing swirl together in his sultry dark eyes. Her own longings rushed back tenfold as she swayed against him.

He kissed her, devouring her mouth, caressing her lips, stealing her breath, suspending all conscious thought. His tongue penetrated and mated with her own, accelerating her pulse, capturing her soul. He felt like spring sunshine after a long winter, as necessary to her existence as food, water and shelter.

Like pleasure personified.

She looped her arms about his neck as his palms slid down her back, pulling her against him, until there wasn't a breath of air between. Burning inside, she arched into him, throwing her head back as his lips descended to nuzzle her neck.

"God, you feel so good, so perfect," he whispered, sending shivers across her skin.

He conquered her lips again, exploring and claiming every inch of her mouth. Juliette pushed her fingers through his thick hair, knowing she should pull away. She didn't.

As if by unspoken agreement, they moved in unison to the couch, lips melding, tongues mating. Mitch sat, positioning Juliette to straddle his hips. Immediately, she felt the solid width of his chest cushioning her...and the thick heat of his erection pressing against her sensitive, swollen sex, silently tempting her.

Juliette had never been a deeply sexual creature. Mitch changed everything.

She moaned into his mouth, luxuriating in her heady freefall into desire. Mitch's hands wandered from her shoulders, down her back, to her hips, inciting her need...breathing life into her fantasy. It wasn't hard to imagine them naked, panting together as he buried himself deep in her and, with those hands guiding her hips, urging her down to take him even deeper.

The very thought made her womb cramp. Moisture rushed

from her body, wetting her black yoga pants. Of all the times she wasn't wearing panties, why did it have to be when she was so aroused?

With hands splayed against her buttocks, he brought her closer, closer—until she could have sworn they were one being. God, this was gloriously insane. It should stop, some corner of her mind said.

But the gentle abrasion of his erection against her sex negated rational thought. She liked Mitch, wanted him...and wanted him to know it. He was everything she shouldn't want. But in that moment, it didn't matter. He cared about her. And somehow, over the course of the last few weeks, she'd come to care about him, too—deeply.

Then Mitch reached through her shirt and cupped her breast, thumbed her turgid nipple. Her flesh sizzled against his fingers. Flash and fire, heat and hedonism all assailed her in rapid-fire reaction.

"Juliette, baby... If this is going to stop, you're going to have to be the strong one. I want you too bad to end this."

His whisper tore through her resistance.

"Don't stop," she gasped in return just before she laid her lips over his and sunk deep into his mouth.

In a matter of moments, Mitch swept her red T-shirt over her head, leaving her top half clad in her sports bra. His fingertips swept over her bare skin, and goose pimples followed. He moaned.

"So damn soft. You're undoing me. Do you know how many times I've wanted you and wondered just how good you'd feel?"

Juliette understood completely since she shared the same affliction.

Before she could say a word, he grabbed at her bra with his

right hand, his left on her hip again, keeping her pressed to his hardness. He pulled her bra over her head and tossed it away from her body.

Wow, he'd gotten it off smoothly. Clearly, he was *way* more experienced than her. What kind of woman was he used to? Someone who knew a thing or two about sex, no doubt. Which was *so* not her.

Mitch took her breasts in his hands, teasing the nipples with his fingers, applying light pressure, teasing brushes...

"Mitch," she gasped.

"God, baby. You're beautiful." He gently pinched her nipple. "Pretty, pink..."

Resisting the urge to arch into his hand, she gasped as a dark swirl of need pooled in her belly. "Wait."

To his credit, he immediately stopped. Completely. His breathing was harsh against her shoulder, his body taut beneath her as he gripped her hips like his lifeline. She felt his heart revving beneath her palm. But he stopped.

"Sorry. Too fast?"

"No. I...just don't want to disappoint you."

He took her face in his hands, arousal on the backburner behind his concern. "How could you think you ever would? I don't ever remember noticing or caring how soft a woman's skin was or how well she fit against me. But you? The details are burned into my brain, baby. And they're lighting me on fire."

His dark stare blazed at her, backing up his words. Juliette bit her lip against a rush of pleasure and pressed on.

"I don't do this a lot," she whispered.

"Have sex with a guy after two dates?"

"Have sex at all." She blushed. "It's been about five years."

Shock crossed his face before he caught and neutralized it.

"You and Brimmley never...?"

She shook her head. "He didn't press."

And she'd never volunteered. Because she'd never wanted him. It was ugly, but it was a fact.

God, could she actually picture herself married to Andrew?

A frown overtook Mitch's face, and Juliette felt her stomach drop to her knees. Of course he was disappointed. She wasn't experienced and probably couldn't keep up with him...

Juliette closed her eyes. "Look, I know you're used to girls who are far more sophisticated and think this sort of thing is no big deal."

"Because sex wasn't a big deal with them. You're totally different. This *is* important."

God, the man consistently surprised her. So often he was just...perfect.

Her eyes flew open and she stared at him, full of wary hope. "Love me."

"Oh, baby, I will." He stroked her hair with tender hands. "I'm going to take such good care of you."

With a quick yank, he whipped his shirt over his head—and her heart stopped. Powerful, lean, sculpted under the dark hair that swirled over his pecs and ran in a trail straight down. He spent a lot of time pushing his body, using it in every way intended obviously. When he moved, he rippled—shoulders, pecs, abs. She'd suspected he was strong and well put together, but this... She swallowed.

"You okay?" he murmured.

Slowly, she nodded and laid a palm on his chest. The muscles jumped beneath her touch.

"Wow," she breathed.

"When you touch me, you have power over me. Don't doubt

it."

She scooted back onto his thighs and whisked a finger down the hard ridges of his abs. Again, he rippled and leapt where she touched. That was potent stuff. She shivered.

Mitch grabbed her wrists. "You're distracting me, and I want to make this right for you. Since you waited so long, I'm going to guess that your last time wasn't great."

"It was over so fast, I couldn't say." She winced.

"Not this time. I've wanted this invitation since the first time I saw you, so I'm going to stay a good, long while."

Juliette had no doubt he could keep that promise. His vow became a shiver that arrowed straight down her belly, between her legs. A part of her knew, just knew, he was going to completely overtake her, overwhelm her. And she loved the anticipation.

With powerful hands, Mitch took hold of her hips again and again brought her against his chest, his sex. She gasped when the hot skin of his solid chest connected with her, sizzling her all over. His mouth followed, finding hers on the first swipe, invading, plundering—owning.

An endless kiss later, Juliette was dizzy and wet and aching. Mitch was going to overwhelm her. She burned to see just how much and how far she'd fall for him.

She mourned his loss when he broke the kiss and took her breasts in his hands again. His thumbs were busy strumming the beaded peaks, and every brush sent a fresh wave of tingles across her skin.

Then he put one in his mouth and sucked.

The world spun away from her. Pleasure spasmed in her belly. More moisture coated her sex. She gripped his shoulders for support, marveling in the back of her mind that she couldn't get her hands around even half of one.

Mitch pulled away with a scrape of his teeth that electrified her before moving to the other and repeating the process. Then he started all over. Juliette moaned, all but clawing at his shoulders as she hung on for dear life.

Never before had she been remotely tempted to rip off a man's pants. Oh, she was so tempted now. Whatever it took to get him closer, deep.

He had similar ideas.

Hooking his thumbs into the waistband of her yoga pants, he pulled down, whisking them over her hips, her butt, her thighs, until they were an afterthought on the floor.

"Oh, holy hell." He looked shell-shocked as his palms roamed from her waist, down her hips, over her bare thighs. "You're killing me. No panties?"

"I just came from a yoga class. Panties just...get in the way."

"I think that's an excellent life philosophy." He caressed the lean line of her hip again. "So damn sexy."

Juliette laughed—until he reclined on the sofa, his back propped up by the back of the couch. Then he arranged her back to his front, her head pillowed on his shoulder. She turned to look at him, and he captured her mouth in a slow, drugging melding of lips and tongues.

When he finally broke the kiss, she was honest-to-goodness panting. A daze of need descended, and she only felt more dizzy when he looped an arm over her waist and set his hand roaming her body—plumping her breast, teasing her nipple, skimming her abdomen, delving lower...right between her legs. Right over her clit.

She sucked in a harsh breath. Even though they weren't

facing each other, the position was more intimate than anything she'd ever experienced.

"You're wet for me, baby. Knowing that is driving me out of my mind."

His touch was driving her out of hers.

Mitch's breathing picked up, and his exhalations on her neck sent shivers through her. His fingers kept driving her higher as he toyed with her, continually rubbing the slick bundle of nerves twitching under the pad of his fingers. Sensations climbed, fast and steady and merciless.

"Amazing," he whispered. "The way you tense and tremble. Your whole body is blushing pink. You're swelling here." He cupped her sex. "Under my hand. Damn."

Orgasm was about to overtake her. He knew exactly how to push her buttons, how to thrill her body...

"Yes," she whimpered, lifting her hips to his hand.

He took the opportunity to swivel her top leg over his, opening her sex more. Then he plunged his fingers deep.

Juliette screamed as the tension ramped up more, higher, until she was a breath from exploding. He teased her with his fingertips, rubbing at a spot so sensitive, she arched to get closer to the touch.

"Baby, I need you. Are you ready?"

She answered with a frantic nod. "Yes. God, yes."

Behind her, she felt his hands fumble, heard the *clink* of his belt buckle coming undone. With a bend and a wiggle, he was every bit as naked as she was.

With a tentative reach behind her, Juliette felt her way up his thigh, then latched on to his erection and squeezed. Encircling him, her fingertips didn't quite touch as she stroked up and down his long length.

Juliette gulped.

Mitch groaned in her ear. "Your touch is amazing."

He thrust into her grip, shuddering and murmuring sounds of pleasure into her ear. Juliette felt the power she had over him, and it aroused her more. Mitch was bigger and more experienced, but at the moment, he was at her mercy. He wanted her. He cared. They mattered.

The thought gave her confidence and warmed her at once.

Feathering his lips across her neck, Mitch smoothed a hand over her breast, down her belly and back onto her clit. The arousal that had taken a momentary breather was back. With a vengeance. It leapt to life as if plugged into a 120 volt socket. With a few strokes of his fingers and the feel of his hard sex in her hand, she was about to have a meltdown.

Her orgasm sizzled, burning right under his fingers, and he knew it. He teased her. With a keening cry, she tightened her fist on him.

Wrapping a hand around her wrist, he drew her fingers away from his erection and eased away from her wet nubbin.

"No..."

"Shh. The first time you come for me, I want to feel it by being deep inside you."

The need inside her torqued, tightened. "Hurry..."

A rustle of cloth, a tear, a moment's hesitation—then she felt the hard tip of him at her entrance.

Condom. It had been so long since she'd had to think of such things. Mitch has so overwhelmed her that she hadn't even stopped to think about the practicalities. "Thank God you're prepared."

"I didn't know if you were on the pill. I want to be careful with you."

Juliette turned her head. "I'm not."

His lips curled up. "Good thing I was a Boy Scout."

A comment that good Boy Scouts were prepared but not necessarily for sex hovered on the tip of her tongue.

The comment dissipated when Mitch grasped her hips and pulled her down as he arched up into her. At the feel of him working his way inside her, reality began to spin away...

A million sensations raced through Mitch as he inched inside Juliette. She melted around him, her flesh slowly yielding, only to clasp him tight. His brain shut down except a few critical thoughts.

Gorgeous. Tight. Giving. Perfect.

Home.

He gripped her hip to anchor him against the crazy rush of need as he pushed deeper inside her. Juliette moaned, and he looked at her flushed face, her sweetly parted lips. He couldn't resist.

Leaning in, he kissed her again, stroking his tongue past her lips. Sweet and tangy. Hot. The most addicting flavor he ever remembered tasting. Mind blowing. He had to get deeper now, mouth and body. Take her completely.

Claim her.

Dangerous thought, since she was all but engaged to someone else. The thought was a machete in the chest, and he normally didn't poach. As he moved in for another kiss, he knew he couldn't give her up. Not yet. He had to have her first. Maybe that would get her out of his system.

And he was so lying to himself.

He tore his mouth away and groaned.

"Mitch," she cried out as he burrowed deeper.

"Right here, baby."

Juliette reached back and caressed his face. Even that one look in her blue eyes was a *zing* to his gut. They were connected: gazes, bodies...hearts. God, how fast was he falling for this woman?

Whatever. It was too late to stop.

Gliding a palm over her breast and back down her belly, he buried his fingers in her damp curls again. She cried out, her skin turning even rosier. Juliette was always beautiful, but aroused... She knocked him on his ass. He couldn't keep his mouth off her. From her lips, down her silky-soft neck, her shoulder, then to that berry nipple begging for attention. Then he started over again.

Around him, the clasp of her sex finally loosened enough to let him in completely, and he sunk deep gratefully and slowly, pausing if she tensed or whimpered. He suspected that she hadn't had many lovers, but now wasn't the time to ask.

Instead, he groaned at the million tingles pelting him. Holding off wasn't going to be easy, but Mitch was determined to make Juliette sigh in satisfaction.

Curling one arm under her and grabbing her top leg in his other, he thrust deep, nudged his lips against her ear and whispered, "I could stay like this with you all night."

Passion burned across that shy expression. Her uncertainty and need mingled, until she practically glowed with a vulnerability that made him want to protect her utterly. Wearing her professional face, Juliette was striking. But being a rosy-cheeked woman, bare to him in every way? She was like nothing he'd ever experienced. She amazed him.

He couldn't hold back another moment.

Before she could say anything, he withdrew almost completely, then drove inside her again. Completely.

She moaned, her fingers fisting in his hair, the little sting somehow arousing.

Again, he repeated the process, nearly leaving the hot clasp of her body, only to thrust his way back in to the hilt, basking in the tight grip she had on him. He gritted his teeth against the rage of pleasure, then nipped at her neck.

"The feel of you is blowing my mind, baby. So hot, and you smell amazing."

She peppered kisses across his cheek and gripped his hair tighter, holding onto the sofa cushion in front of her for dear life as he rocked into her once more.

Damn, being with her was so hot, like nothing he'd ever experienced. The only thing that would make it better...

Mitch propped her top leg on top of his, then cupped her sex again with his free hand. He strummed his fingers over clit, loving the way she arched and mewled. And begged.

"Please..." Her whisper was potent, going straight to his erection. "Please, Mitch."

His skin felt itchy and tight as desire consumed more and more of him, but he didn't stop his deep, rhythmic thrusts inside her. She clawed at the couch, at his scalp, her panting breaths heating his skin, her moans running like shivers down his spine.

Under his fingers, her bundle of nerves swelled, turned hard. All around him, she tightened, moaned, and let loose, her cry echoing off the ceiling.

Gritting his teeth, Mitch resisted the urge to follow her over—barely. Pleasure rushed up his erection. It would be so easy to let go... But he sucked it up and held it in, reciting his ABCs backward to distract himself. He refused to disappoint her.

When her breathing slowed and her body fell limp against him, he slowed his pace and pressed kisses along her neck and the side of her breast.

"Oh, wow," she breathed.

He wasn't really in a laughing mood, but her words earned her a chuckle. "I'm thinking that's a good sign."

"The best," she assured, then bit her lip. "I've never..."

"Orgasmed?"

She nodded and ducked her head shyly, the tangle of her blonde hair sliding over her shoulders, down his chest. "Not with anyone else."

Suddenly, he felt ten feet tall and ready to make sure he was the only one she experienced such satisfaction with.

"Seriously?"

Juliette hesitated, then nodded. "Seriously. I just never got that much into sex before."

"I'm totally into you." He thrust deep. "Literally. Can you take more?"

"Take it? I would plead for it."

He smiled and pushed a lock of hair from her cheek. "Listening to that would be pure pleasure, but I don't want to wait to feel you again."

Quickly, he withdrew, eased her to her back, fell between her thighs and filled her in one thrust.

Her gasp mixed with his groan. Electric need burned across his skin and deep in his gut as they touched chest to chest, belly to belly. Damn, this woman got to him. Fast, going right to his head like a potent brew.

"Mitch, please..."

Not about to keep Juliette waiting, he set a teeth-gritting

pace. Too fast to ignore, but too slow to appease the monster need roaring inside him. It was just right to provide her maximum friction.

She dug her nails into his back and panted in his ear, dusting his neck and shoulders with nipping little kisses that hyped him up even more.

"You're greedy," he teased.

Not even trying to deny it, she nodded and threw her hips up at him, meeting his thrust on pace. Oh, hell. That was...wow. It would do him in fast. He had to get her there with him before he lost it.

Tilting her up more, he changed the angle of his thrust and dragged slowly inside her until she moaned his name.

With a smile, he did it again.

"Mitch!" She clutched at him as she cried out and tightened around him.

"Need it now? Need me?"

Her nod was a frantic bobbing of her head, but he understood perfectly. And couldn't wait to give her what she wanted.

Mitch went into overdrive, pouring on the steam, plunging into her over and over and over.

Her moan became a keening cry. She tensed, clamped down on him, her mouth frantic against his neck, jaw, cheek. Then she screamed and pulsed and blew him away.

Shouting and gripping her tight, like he'd never let go, Mitch released and held her close, as if there was no tomorrow.

Despite the pleasure that had just passed between them, he knew there might not be.

The ringing of a telephone penetrated Juliette's haze of

afterglow a moment later. She decided to ignore it and let Mitch continue to stroke her back with his tender touch.

When it rang again, he paused. “Do you need to get that?”

Juliette considered kissing him again in answer, then realized Kara was a little late coming home. “I better get it, just in case my sister’s undependable car has broken down again.”

On wobbly knees, Juliette grabbed her clothes and crossed the floor. She reached the phone on the fourth ring and inhaled deeply, trying to return the normalcy to breathing. Lord, that man could make her feel so alive and desired!

All too aware of Mitch’s heavy, sexy stare, Juliette covered her nakedness with her clothes and lifted the receiver. “Hello?”

“Darling, great news!” a familiar voice exclaimed without preamble.

“Andrew?” Her voice seemed strangled even to her own ears. She cast a nervous glance at Mitch, who sat back on the couch and whispered something that sounded like a four-letter word.

Andrew laughed. “Were you expecting someone else?”

She touched her fingertips to her swollen lips. It wasn’t fair to deceive a man who had been nothing but kind and supportive to her. Yet she didn’t know what else to do. With Mitch in the room and a handful of days before Christmas wasn’t the time to tell Andrew what had happened here tonight. Plus, she couldn’t see straight when every nerve in her body ached to touch the man who sat a mere ten feet away.

“No. Well, I thought you might be Kara,” she amended, casting a nervous glance at Mitch. “I haven’t seen her yet tonight.”

“She’ll turn up. Listen...”

Juliette did so with half an ear as she watched Mitch rise

from the couch, dispose of the condom, stretch, his glorious nudity completely distracting. The man had sexy everything.

"I have good news. We made a major breakthrough in negotiations today, which means I might be able to come home early."

That got her attention. "Early?"

"Yes, isn't that great? We can get on with our future that much sooner."

"How early?"

Juliette heard the panic in her voice. Andrew must have heard it, too. His voice cooled considerably. "I'll have to let you know. Nothing is firm yet."

"I see. Well," she said awkwardly. "Let me know."

"I'll call when I know something for sure," he said, then hung up.

Juliette laid the receiver in its cradle in pensive silence and excused herself to the bathroom and flipped on the light.

Oh, God. Hair in disarray, mouth swollen, whisker burns on her neck, smudged mascara and dazed eyes... She looked like a woman who had just crawled out of bed with a sex god—which he was—who'd given her multiple orgasms—which he had. She wanted to cry, but that was useless. Instead, she tossed on her clothes and tried to fix her appearance. In the back of her mind, though, was the realization that she was completely hooked on a man so wrong for her and could muster no enthusiasm for the man who, at least on paper, should be her Prince Charming. What was she going to do? She couldn't keep seeing them both; it wasn't fair to either one.

But which one? There was no easy answer.

Hesitantly, she exited the bathroom to find Mitch zipping up his jeans. He threw his black tee over his head again and finger-combed his hair.

"Brimmley's coming home soon?"

Juliette nodded, searching his face for traces of anger or any other emotion. All she saw was a tinge of anger and faint regret before Mitch looked away with a whispered curse.

With the jangle of keys outside, Kara pushed the front door open and waltzed into the room, full of smiles. "Hey there."

Her sister's gaze bounced between her and Mitch. Then her smile got wider.

Kara was no idiot. She knew *exactly* what had gone on here.

Wishing a big hole would open up and swallow her, Juliette made brief introductions.

After a cordial handshake, Mitch said, "I think I'd better go."

"Don't run off on my account," Kara insisted, backing toward the hall, her eyes knowing. "I was just going to my room to...um, listen to music. It'll be loud. I won't hear a thing."

"It was nice meeting you," he said as Kara slammed her bedroom door. With a sigh, he turned to Juliette. "I know you have a lot to think about. I have to be honest and say that I don't want what we have to be over."

She didn't either. Biting her lip, she struggled for words. "But I don't know if we make sense together."

"We made great sense less than an hour ago," he pointed out in frustration. "You told me yourself that you can't share your body with someone you don't care about. And what happened between us... You didn't hold back anything from me. Yet you haven't gone to bed with Brimmley and you don't seem in a hurry to. I don't think it's hard to do the math on this one."

"It isn't that simple."

"Yeah, it is. You're clinging to someone who can't make you happy because you're chasing a guarantee that life doesn't offer."

Did he really think that? "I'm not! I want more for myself and my kids than a collection of well-used moving boxes. Can you swear we'd never move?"

"Of course not."

"Then I don't know how we can ever work this out."

"I think we could, but you're too damn scared to try. I'm man enough to admit that I'm falling for you. But I won't promise you something unrealistic to keep you. Think about whether you'd rather have stability or love. Call me when you decide."

Juliette closed her eyes to avoid watching Mitch's departure. But she heard it, the soft click of her front door, his heavy footsteps descending the stairs.

She wanted to cry. Her life was falling apart. Andrew might return to town earlier than planned. He'd be expecting an answer to his marriage proposal. *Now* she understood passion. Mitch had proven that Andrew could never make her blood race, and she sensed that after Mitch, she wouldn't be happy with anything less. Yet if she followed her heart and chose the gorgeous reporter, the decision might fill her life with nothing but moving and misery.

What a catch-22.

Juliette sat in her office the next morning, contemplating her future, in between remembrances of Mitch's touch.

What a tangle.

Maybe she should tell Andrew that she needed more time

to decide. Marriage was a huge step, and they hadn't been dating very long.

But Andrew was ready for his wife, a picket fence and his two point two children now. If she put him off much longer, he would no doubt take his supportive, stable demeanor elsewhere.

At the very least, she owed him an explanation about her behavior recently. And...he deserved to know what had happened between her and Mitch last night.

Dreading the coming conversation, she lifted the telephone receiver and punched out Andrew's office number in Milwaukee.

After a few rings, he answered.

"Hi, Andrew," she said quietly.

"Hello."

"How's it going today? The meeting still progressing?"

"Better than expected, yes."

She bit her lip at his clipped tone. "Is it still cold up there?"

"This is Wisconsin in December. It's a balmy eighteen, with a wind chill of four degrees."

Neither Andrew's description of Wisconsin's weather, nor his unwelcoming tone left her with a warm, fuzzy feeling. "How does anyone live there?"

"I have no idea and I don't plan on finding out. Why did you call? Not to talk about this lousy weather, I'm sure."

An awkward silence followed. She sighed. "No, I called to tell you something."

"Hmmm. It doesn't sound as if I'm going to like what you have to say."

"Probably not. You know I've dated that guy from *The Signal*, Mitch MacKinnon?" At Andrew's grunt, she said, "He was at my place yesterday when you called."

"Was he there on business or pleasure?"

"Business...originally. Then he kissed me. I—I kissed him back. That's not the first time it's happened. And that's not all that happened. I wanted to be honest with you."

Andrew said nothing for a full minute. His short, angry breaths came across the line, filling Juliette with guilt. "You painted the town red with him, then you fucked him. Is that what you're trying to say?"

Since Andrew rarely cursed, Juliette recoiled. "Andrew, it's not like I planned what happened."

"So you let this slick reporter seduce you. I purposely haven't pushed you for sex. I've been patient because you seemed skittish. The minute I turn my back..." He paused, and she could hear teeth gnashing. "Why the hell did you let him into your bed?"

"I'm not exactly sure. We have good chemistry. Maybe more. I don't know."

"Chemistry? Are you going to throw away what we could have over something that fleeting?"

"I have feelings for him," she confessed. "I think they're mutual, but—"

"Feelings? We're so perfectly suited, what you feel for him can only be infatuation. Don't you know that?"

"I don't know anything right now."

He cursed. "Does this mean you're not going to marry me?"

"You still want to marry me?"

"I don't love what you've done, but I love you. I would accept your vow that it would never happen again if you'll say yes to my proposal."

It was good Andrew wasn't throwing a huge jealous tizzy—

but part of her wanted him to. He wasn't completely incensed she had shared every part of her body with another man she'd known a mere two weeks?

"I haven't made any decisions yet," she murmured.

"Damn it, you owe me an answer." She heard him pound on some solid surface.

"I need more time to untangle my thoughts. I'm just not ready—"

"But you were ready to do the horizontal mambo with a guy you barely know," he growled in frustration. "When will you be ready?"

Juliette tried not to get angry in return. After all, his points were valid. And guilt was eating her alive. The last thing in the world she wanted to do was hurt such a great guy.

"When you get home, I'll have an answer, like I promised."

"Well, I'm coming home early. In two days, to be exact. I'll expect your answer then. And hope you're smart enough not to throw away a great future together for a fling."

Juliette heard a click, followed by dial tone. Two days? The thought of deciding the course of her future in two days was enough to make her stomach turn over. What would she do?

At six-thirty that evening, Juliette headed for home. Her brain had ceased to think of anything but Mitch and Andrew and her decision hours ago.

She parked in front of her apartment, searching for Kara's car. She didn't find it. Stepping out of her own car, she thanked God for any peace and quiet she could get tonight. Eyelids heavy, she scooped up her briefcase and headed up the stairs to her apartment.

She stopped short at the sight of a man with graying hair and a black overcoat loitering on her landing. She grabbed her cell phone in her pocket, just in case.

She climbed another stair, her keys thrust between her fingers for protection. At the sound of her heels clicking against the cement, the man turned.

"Daddy?" Her eyes widened. Her mouth fell open. "Daddy, what are you doing here?"

He cocked a half-smile and cast his gaze to the ground. Gosh, he still shuffled his feet, even though he looked older. In fact, the creases around his mouth and eyes lent him a dejected look.

"I got a letter from your sister." He held up a ragged white envelope. "She said she missed me and wondered why I'd forgotten her birthday again."

Hope, disbelief, fear—all threaded around each other and through her at once. She stared at him and swallowed.

"Can I come in?" he asked.

Aware again that they were standing outside in the December chill, she pushed her front door open. "Of course."

They entered, and Juliette closed the door behind her. Her father glanced around, scanning the living room and kitchen.

"Nice place," he commented. "Do you and Kara live here together?"

She nodded. "How did you get here so quickly? Did you take leave?"

"Not exactly." He shuffled his feet again. Juliette frowned at his nervous habit. "I retired last month."

"What? *You* retired?"

"I had a heart attack."

A gasp escaped her. *Dad?* She'd always thought him

invincible, able to leap tall buildings in a single bound and all that.

"Oh my God," she murmured. "When? Why didn't you call us?"

"About two months ago." He reached out to pat her shoulder. "It was a mild one, so I didn't want to worry you girls. But a heart attack makes you stop and think. I had to reevaluate my priorities."

"What do you mean?"

"I didn't know what I wanted out of the rest of my life. It's been years since I had considered LATAF."

She raised a brow. "I didn't think you would ever opt for any 'Life After The Air Force'."

He shrugged. "It's real simple: after weeks of hideous bed rest, I realized ambition and a promotion every two years couldn't take the place of family."

Juliette felt her jaw drop to her chest. "You figured that out?"

"I know it's a little late." He sighed. "Hell, it's a lot too late. But I always loved you and Kara. I just wasn't the best at showing it."

She stared at her father in silence, words escaping her. Did he want reassurance, or just to speak his mind? He couldn't want to start over. She'd outgrown adolescence years ago.

"What made you come here?"

"I know it's sudden and that I should have called first, but I just want to explain something to you, maybe take you two to dinner." He smiled. "I've got your sister's birthday gift, too. After that...we'll see."

Wow. That was more parenting than he'd done in the last five years. The angry half of her wanted to turn him away. After all, where had he been when she'd needed him years ago? Commanding raids and playing Air Force politics.

But turning him away might mean risking her only chance at having a relationship with her father...and healing past wounds.

"All right. Take a seat." She pointed to the couch, then sat in the nearby chair. "I'm listening."

"Well, I—ah..." He squeezed his eyes shut and rubbed his hands together in a nervous gesture. "Damn it, I loved your mother. And after she died, nowhere felt like home. God, I didn't want you girls to have the childhood I had, wondering if you'd have enough to eat or shoes for the winter. But you got so good at looking after Kara that I sometimes felt in the way."

His honesty touched Juliette. "We needed you. I was a child raising a child."

"I know. I was too lost in my problems to see yours." He turned his gaze down to his shoes. "I don't think I ever told you this. I never wanted you to know. But I came from Brooklyn, the streets that weren't good. A lot of the guys I grew up with spent their lives in prison.

"At eighteen, I'd decided I was going to be somebody, maybe even a hero. I joined the Air Force. Shortly after that, I met your mother, a captain's daughter."

"Daddy, I don't understand—"

"I owe you at least an explanation," he said, then stood and paced to the kitchen table. "Your mother was beautiful. You look a lot like her. Anyway, I always wanted her to be proud of me. After she was gone, Uncle Sam's demands were all I could deal with. I didn't know what to do with grief. Even though I knew moving was inevitable, I forgot that slapping up four walls around you two kids didn't make it a home."

"You were an absent father before she died," Juliette

pointed out. "Moving was only part of the problem."

"You're right. I was just an enlisted man. If I hadn't been so concerned about my career and afraid I'd lose your mother's respect if I didn't excel, I could have been a better father. Fear kept me down. I wasn't afraid of dying; I was afraid of failing. Then your mother died..." He paused, then lifted his gaze to her again, his blue eyes bleak with regret. "I know all the what-ifs and should-have-beens don't change the fact I was an absentee father at best. I'm sorry."

Her years of resentment suddenly felt petty, yet so difficult to let go of. "Why are you telling me this now?"

He shrugged. "I feel guilty, as long as we're being honest. I want to make the past up to you, if possible. Plus, now that I'm getting older, I want family around me, and you girls are my only blood. Can you give an old guy a chance to rectify his mistakes?"

Juliette frowned. How many times had she dreamed of hearing these words from her dad? A thousand, at least. Now that he had said them, what was she supposed to do? Forgive him? Holding a grudge felt natural, if immature. But giving him a taste of his own medicine would solve nothing. If he wanted a real father-daughter rapport, the least she could do was try.

"All right. Did you have anything in mind?" she asked.

"I'd like to see more of you. A buddy of mine settled in the Valley. I'll stay with him and his wife until I find a place of my own." He paced back to the sofa. "But I'd like to get to know you and Kara again, make up for lost time in whatever way I can. Is that all right?"

"We'd like that."

He smiled, his expression so bittersweet, a poignant chord sounded in Juliette. She swiped at her tears with her fingers and sniffled.

"Can an old guy have a hug?" He held open his arms.

Juliette walked into them and held tight.

He drew in a deep breath. The sound resonated with relief. "I love you. Can I say that to my grown daughter?"

She nodded. "Welcome home, Daddy."

With her father's arms around her, the world felt almost perfect. But a piece of the puzzle seemed out of her reach, creating a gaping hole in the center of a euphoric picture.

Mitch's laughing face and dancing dimples sprang to mind.

ଊ

Christmas morning dawned bright and balmy. In keeping with family tradition, Juliette, Kara and their father hung blinking white lights and a wreath on her front door that morning. The suddenly warmer weather dictated they wear summer shorts and T-shirts. Kara and their father laughed about California's great winter weather.

Juliette smiled wanly in response.

Where was her Christmas spirit? She put the last bulb in place and descended the ladder to stand on the balcony and frowned. Perhaps the seventy-five degree weather was inhibiting her holiday cheer. After all, southern California wasn't exactly a winter wonderland.

But last year's weather had been much the same and it hadn't affected her joy in the holiday. No, it was the fact that today was D-Day.

Andrew's trip had been unexpectedly delayed. He'd arrived at LAX late last night. He had called a few minutes ago to say he was on his way over to her place—and was expecting an answer.

She still didn't have one to give him.

And Mitch had all but disappeared. She was both relieved and piqued that he hadn't come by or called. His seductive presence would have been a total distraction...but she missed him and that easy-dimpled smile, the way he could make her feel like the sexiest woman alive with just a kiss...never mind the memories of what they'd done on her sofa.

None of that added up to resolution, however.

For days, she'd been struggling to think logically, but all she'd been able to grasp was a confusing tangle of longings and gut reactions. Unfortunately, she hadn't come across any great article in *Cosmo* recently telling her whether she should marry the man who made her insides quiver or the one who was prepared to give her the life she craved. Her horoscope hadn't even been much help.

Juliette sighed as she watched her sister and father tease each other. Daddy was a changed man, and Kara was responding as if she'd been thirsty for parental love. Juliette smiled as her father cast her a concerned look. She waved for good measure.

What was Mitch doing today? Juliette stared at the limited view of Santa Clarita available from her balcony. Where beneath the ever-present film of brownish smog was he? Was he thinking of her? Missing her?

A honking horn jolted Juliette back to the here and now. Andrew pulled up and began unloading a trunkful of gifts from his BMW.

Screeching like a child, Kara raced down the stairs, to the parking lot. She bestowed a quick hug upon Andrew, then grabbed handfuls of the packages. Andrew watched mutely as the younger Lowell darted upstairs to the apartment.

Juliette ambled down to the parking lot, pasting on a smile.

"Isn't she like a four-year-old at Christmas?"

Andrew nodded. "I've missed you."

"It's good to see you," she said, vaguely aware her feelings didn't match her words. She stepped out of his embrace and turned her attention to the remaining gifts in his trunk when he tried to kiss her.

Andrew took her arm and turned her to face him. "Are you turning me down?"

"Let's not talk about this in the parking lot on Christmas morning." She turned away again and headed for the stairs.

"Do you have something you want to tell me?" he asked, his voice strained. "I've waited, God knows..."

He had, and she felt guilty as hell that she still didn't know what to say. "Let's get these presents upstairs."

He raced around her and took the packages from her arms, effectively halting her. "Give me the best Christmas present of all. Say you'll marry me."

Juliette opened her mouth, to say what, she wasn't sure. Her father striding down the stairs toward them saved her having to answer.

Juliette introduced Andrew to her father, the trio mounted the stairs to her apartment. Just inside her front door, Andrew stopped her again.

"Please. Say something. I can't take the waiting anymore."

"Let's wait until we're alone. After we've opened the gifts and had dinner, we'll go for a walk."

Andrew loosed a frustrated sigh and gritted his teeth but said nothing.

In the living room, Juliette and the others deposited gifts around the tree.

"Wow." Her father stared at the tree. "This is sure a

bountiful Christmas. If you had many more gifts stuffed beneath that over-decorated tree, you wouldn't have room to walk in here."

Kara dropped the popcorn she'd been stringing to add to the tree and began passing out gifts. "Isn't it great!"

Laughing at her sister, Juliette turned on the radio. Bing Crosby's smooth tones filled the room with a Christmas classic.

Kara was right. Today should be great. Her father and sister looked so happy. Having Daddy here as a real father was an unexpected blessing. Why couldn't she get into the spirit?

She wished Mitch was here.

"Darling, would you make me some coffee?" Andrew called, interrupting her thoughts.

"Okay." But she wondered why he couldn't do it himself. Even his first time over, Mitch hadn't expected her to wait on him. He'd simply inquired as to the whereabouts of her drinking glasses and given her time to gather her belongings. He'd even thoughtfully brought breakfast.

She wondered if Mitch was spending the day with his mother. Had he received the CD of Tchaikovsky's famous ballets she'd mailed to his office earlier in the week?

An ache centered in her abdomen. She couldn't write off the pang to simple lack of food since she'd been stress-eating cookies and eggnog all morning.

Damn, she missed Mitch.

"Open this." Andrew handed her a box, snaring her attention. Its shape was a large rectangle, somewhat heavy. "I have a feeling you'll love it."

Juliette shot him a smile before turning her attention to the red-wrapped box. After tearing the paper away, she opened the lid to find a downy royal blue winter coat.

"A coat," she stated the obvious for lack of a catchier phrase. "It's nice."

"Isn't that the one you said you liked when we were at the mall before I left?" he asked, seemingly perplexed.

Andrew thought of her in enough romantic light to buy her a coat. "This is the coat I mentioned. I know I'll use it. Thanks."

He frowned. "You don't like it?"

"No, I do. Why don't you open your gifts?"

Andrew did, and seemed equally puzzled with her selection of leather gloves, aftershave, shirts and ties.

"Thanks," he said, wearing a strained smile.

What was happening? They'd always known each other so well, she'd thought. Yet here they were buying the kind of gifts one usually purchased for a sibling or parent, instead of a lifelong mate. Nothing here romantic at all.

"Here." Her father handed her a large box with a silky green bow. Juliette scanned the tag. "Another one to Juliette from Andrew."

She pasted on a smile and hummed with a carol on the radio, as she slowly peeled away the bright Santa-laden paper to reveal a box filled with cookware.

Cookware? They weren't even engaged, and he was already giving her things for the kitchen? "How...practical."

"They're the best, I'm told. Mom swears by these. She says you'll love them."

Juliette stared at Andrew. Hadn't he picked up on the fact she didn't enjoy cooking? In fact, what she created in the kitchen could barely be called edible.

Her gifts to him suggested she didn't know him any better, either.

Chapter Nine

A knock sounded at the door in the next moment. Still frowning, Juliette rose. Who could that be? She wasn't expecting anyone else on Christmas Day.

After rounding the corner from the living room to the front door, she opened the portal to find a petite Italian-looking woman holding a bright gold box with a festive ribbon. A red scarf tied back her dark hair. Her uncertain smile displayed hauntingly familiar dimples.

"Can I help you?" she asked, peering at the woman.

The woman smiled and extended her hand. "Yes. I'm Gianna MacKinnon, Mitch's mother. And you are Juliette." She smiled. "He said you are beautiful. He is right."

"Thank you." She opened the door wider and glanced around the corner hopefully. "Come in. Is Mitch with you?"

The woman stepped back. "No, I did not come to stay, and he would kill me if he knew I was here. I told him I was going to look for a grocery store that was open today." She thrust the box in her hands toward Juliette. "I came to give you this."

Juliette accepted the gift with numb fingers. "This?"

She nodded. "Something Mitch bought for you last week. Then the other day he decides not to give it to you."

The other day—after his abrupt departure. "He did?" She

frowned. “Do you know why?”

The older woman shrugged. “He mumbled something about not interfering in your decisions. But I could not stand to see him mope anymore.” She smiled and reached for Juliette’s hand. “I will ask you to call him, just once. Maybe you can make him smile. Then I promise to poke my nose out of your business.”

In the background, Juliette heard Kara and her father singing the familiar verses of “Jingle Bells”. She studied Gianna’s dark, wise eyes. “Okay.”

“You seem like a sweet girl,” the woman said in a lilting, old-world voice she backed up with a smile. Now Juliette knew where Mitch had inherited the ability to melt her knees with a single grin. “And he is enjoying his Tchaikovsky. *Ciao.*”

“Good bye, Gianna,” she said, then shut the door.

“Who was that?” Andrew asked, rounding the corner from the living room. His gaze fell to the box in her hands.

She bit her lip and waited for the storm. “Mitch MacKinnon’s mother.”

“You’re friends with the man’s *mother*? Did she get you that gift?”

“No. Mitch did.”

She turned her back to Andrew and dashed to the kitchen table to open her gift in private. Even there, she couldn’t be alone. Her father stood beside the cabinet, pouring himself a refill of coffee.

“So you’re still seeing him?” Andrew demanded, following her.

“Not since…that night. Whatever happens, he’s still a friend.”

That much was true, but she omitted telling Andrew about

the gift she'd sent to Mitch. Now wasn't the time.

It was true, but the exclusion felt like a gargantuan jet black fib.

"A friend, is he? So what does one 'friend' send another?" He grabbed and lifted the box, frowning. "It's heavy."

Juliette snatched it back. "I'll open this later."

"Why so secretive, darling?" His voice held an edge.

"No reason."

"Then why don't you open it and find out?" His suggestion felt more like a command.

Juliette gritted her teeth. "Fine."

She tore off the bright bow and paper. Beneath lay a square box with a white background and a picture of a couple inline skating on the front.

"Skates?" Andrew piped up, his voice perplexed. "What a silly gift."

Juliette laughed and tore open the box with a smile. "Oh, this is great! I love to skate on these things."

He rolled his eyes. "Surely you've outgrown something that juvenile."

"It's fun." Her voice held a sharp edge. "If fact, I found the experience quite freeing."

"You can't possibly mean to skate on those things in public?" Andrew asked in horror, as if she'd said she was contemplating shaving her head.

"It's fun and good exercise."

"Tennis is good exercise," Andrew corrected. "Inline skating is so...junior high. What will people say?"

"I haven't been skating in years," her father chimed in. "I'll go with you, if you want. I always loved it, too."

"Thanks, Daddy. That would be great."

"Don't ask me to go with you. I won't be seen doing something that ridiculous," Andrew said and withdrew from the kitchen.

"I wouldn't dream of it," Juliette called after him.

Once he had gone, she removed her skates from the box and rolled one of the wheels with her finger. Even looking at the skates reminded her of Mitch.

"You know," her father said. "Your mother and I didn't always have the easiest time at marriage. She was independent, kind of like you."

Juliette nodded, determined not to show her embarrassment. After all, she and her "boyfriend" had just argued. What must he think?

"Remember the time I told her to quit the bridge club because it took her away from home too much?" he prompted.

"Yes."

Her father broke out into a shoulder-shaking laugh. "So what did she do? Moved the club to our house. That was worse, because then I had to watch you kids and listen to the gossip of the officers' wives."

"You have to admit, it was pretty clever," she said.

"It was. And I learned a valuable lesson. Your mother was her own person, with likes and dislikes and thoughts and feelings. As her husband, I had no right to control any of those, particularly since I was gone from home so often."

Juliette fell silent. She heard the inference in her father's speech to herself and Andrew.

"I should have never believed I had the right to take enjoyment out of her life. She wasn't hurting anyone."

Juliette hugged the skates to her chest. "Andrew is sweet

most of the time. He just doesn't understand anything...frivolous."

"And you've always loved everything whimsical," her father said. "When you were in second grade, you went without lunch so you could glue your dimes and quarters to a piece of gold construction paper you'd gotten from school and make yourself a crown."

Juliette remembered with a smile. "I had that crown a long time."

"I scolded you, remember? Your mother took me aside later and explained that you were just expressing yourself. She said if you had been really hungry, you would have spent your money."

"She was right."

"I admit I wasn't the greatest at showing it, but I loved you. So I made up my mind to accept that part of you, and every other part. If Andrew can't do the same, honey, you might start asking yourself why."

Why?

The single word haunted her while they waited through the early afternoon for dinner. Other discomforting facts loomed as well. She couldn't remember the last time she'd enjoyed Andrew's company. It hadn't been recently. Also disconcerting was the fact that most of her evenings out with him also included her sister—and she preferred it that way.

Her sex life with Andrew had been purposely non-existent. But after two dates with Mitch, she'd thrown caution to the wind and happily gotten naked with him. She wanted to do it again. Andrew had never tempted her like that. In fact, she couldn't recall thinking about Andrew and sex in the same thought.

Why?

Because she didn't love Andrew.

Ouch. An uncomfortable truth...but an important one. They had no business getting married.

The acknowledgement rocked her need for stability to its core.

What had happened to her seemingly perfect future married to a presumably perfect man?

Her relationship with Andrew had all been a mirage, one her fear of risks fed with every heartbeat. Mitch had helped her to see that marrying a man she didn't love would never make her happy. Nor would it be terribly secure.

After all, if she married Andrew, he could eventually fall in love with someone else. Knowing him, he would make himself, and her inadvertently, miserable just to avoid the ugliness of a divorce. Such a legal dissolution of their marriage would be too unsightly for Andrew's palate and profession.

She sighed. Christmas was a lousy time to make the toughest decision of her life. She should be in the holiday spirit. Her father had come, and all was well between them. While his presence added a measure of joy, this...wrongness between her and Andrew threw a note of apprehension in the mix.

Sipping coffee from her cup, she peeked at the turkey in the oven. In the corner, she saw the box containing her new in-line skates. They reminded her of Mitch.

She didn't like her future dangling like a wind chime in a hurricane. After all, Mitch was the reason she'd begun to examine her future. With tingling kisses, killer dimples and challenging words, he'd sunk under her skin and into her heart.

She loved him.

Shock pinged through her. How had it happened? When? Why?

He infuriated her—often. Their vision of the future seemed as diametrically opposed as the North and South Poles. But she ached to touch him. She always felt alive when she was with him. Mitch took her through a gamut of emotions: joy, anger, desire, pride, fear, need... That definitely meant something more than casual attraction.

Even if she and Mitch didn't work out their differences, she was grateful he'd opened her eyes to the fact that marrying Andrew would be a mistake.

But she did want to work it out with Mitch. The fact he seemed to care for her too, that she could easily picture them married, had experienced her matchmaking intuition around him, could only mean she felt the real thing for Mitch.

The rightness of the truth warmed her like a roaring fire in winter. But how would Andrew take her decision? Though they hadn't started dating right away, he'd befriended her when she first moved to Santa Clarita without knowing a soul. He had been her rock through lonely and difficult times. Somehow she had to explain that as spouses, they'd be no good for each other.

ɷ

With a heavy sigh, Juliette removed the picture of Andrew and herself from her desk. Last night had been nothing short of disaster. She'd tried to sprinkle her refusal of his proposal with positive comments and words of friendship. But the look on his face told her the only word he'd heard was "no".

But her future was now hers. Even if their parting had

been more bitter than sweet, the rightness of her decision not to marry Andrew filled her with vivacity and hope.

Now she just hoped Mitch wanted to put the finishing touches on her happy new life by being a part of it.

With trembling fingers, she dialed Mitch's number to tell him what was in her heart. Besides, she'd promised his mother that she would call.

Fantasy flashes of Mitch's jubilant response when she told him of her decision popped through her mind—until his answering machine picked up. "I'm not here. Leave a message." *Beep.*

Juliette left him a quick greeting, then set the phone down with a sigh. She tried his office at *The Signal* next, only to be told he wasn't in.

That man! Here she was, ready to throw caution to the wind and explore the feelings between them, and he was nowhere to be found.

She took a quick trek to The Brunchery, hoping that would take her mind off the waiting. After buying a cup of cappuccino to rev up her coffee buzz, she bought today's edition of *The Signal* and ran back to her office. Maybe reading Mitch's article would occupy her mind.

Behind closed doors, she opened the paper. Almost immediately, she found the catchy headline Mitch had written:

Playing with Matches by Mitchell E. MacKinnon.

Juliette swallowed at the ominous title. The night they'd made love, Mitch had led her to believe he'd written something very neutral, almost benign. He wouldn't mislead her, right?

"Play with matches, and you might get burned" goes the old saying. Unfortunately, for a thirty-three year old Santa Clarita man, that adage proved true.

His trouble began three short months ago, when he became a client of local dating service, A Perfect Match. His story ends with a robbery of major proportions.

According to the victim, Joseph Tarton, he joined A Perfect Match after moving to Santa Clarita from Oregon this summer. "I just wanted to meet people," said Tarton. "It's not easy for me to get acquainted with women. I thought Juliette (Lowell, the service's owner) could help."

Indeed, on December 8, Joe met a woman he'll never forget, one who called herself Rita Young. Mr. Tarton described her as shy and unpretentious. They went out, had Japanese food and went back to his home for coffee.

He woke to discover that Rita had laced his coffee with a sedative and taken every valuable possession in his home, including his credit cards. Later, he learned Rita Young's real name is Rexelle Kramer and that she's wanted in Texas and Florida for similar crimes. So far, police have not located her whereabouts.

Mr. Tarton admits that, had Ms. Lowell inquired about any possible criminal record when he joined the service, he would have been insulted. Today, he says he wishes desperately that he'd never met Rita/Rexelle and that Ms. Lowell had offended him—and every other respondent—with more questions about their criminal backgrounds, followed by a records check. According to Tarton, he's learned since the incident that anything less is careless.

Those contemplating joining a dating service like A Perfect Match need not panic, however. L.A. County's Deputy Sheriff, Thomas Maines, said that this premeditated type of crime doesn't happen often. However, just like anyone answering a singles' advertisement, people should be wary of strangers. Being burned is always a risk when playing with matches.

Juliette rose sightlessly, shock thrumming through every finger and toe. Mitch had actually written that? And he thought it benign?

This sounded like more than just doing his job. He'd actually intimated that she was inept and her questionnaire inadequate. Neither of those accusations had been stated for the reader, but still...

Grabbing the paper from her desk, she stared at his article in disbelief, then slammed it into the trash can by her feet.

He hadn't boldly printed that she was incompetent and her business a hoax. But even a blind man could read between the lines and discern Mitch's insinuation.

Why had he written something so maligning? She was willing to gamble her future on a man like Mitch, despite their different outlooks. He'd seemed so caring, so interested in her. This article read like a stab in the back.

Had she misjudged him and his feelings? He had to have known this would hurt her. Had he...used her?

She bit her lip, holding in tears. Maybe his career and the adventures it would bring were more important than her feelings, after all.

The hellish day crawled by. Business had been slow again. Even some of her own clients had called for reassurance. Anxiety and disappointment knotted her stomach, stunting her ability to think logically. Worst of all, she couldn't understand why she cared about a man whose poison pen could clearly destroy her business. He hadn't called in days now, and she was torn between wanting to touch him and wanting to flay him alive with her tongue.

Under gray, drizzly skies, she returned to her office from lunching on a salad she couldn't force herself to eat. As she yearned for and dreaded, she had a message from Mitch.

She couldn't talk to him now. Hurt and anger would rule her words. She wanted to get calm, center, before talking to him so they could speak rationally. As it stood now, she was an emotional jumble who was likely to scream or cry.

She pitched the pink slip into her wastebasket and ignored the stab of foolish hope running rampant in her heart. And tried to put the whole thing out of her head.

Near five o'clock, Connie stepped into the room wearing a grimace. Poor thing had been walking on eggshells all afternoon. Juliette made a resolution to be extra pleasant to her receptionist.

She popped on her plastic smile. "Hi, Connie. What's up?"

The older woman's grimace stretched into a frown. "There's someone here to see you. I'm going home."

Connie turned and high-tailed herself down the hall. Normally, Juliette might have found her behavior amusing. Today, she couldn't think of anything that made her happy.

She smoothed the lapels of her jacket and reapplied a coat of lipstick, in case her guest was a new client...or a current one in need of reassurance.

Leaving her office behind, she strolled down the hall, a smile pasted on her lips. When she reached the lobby, she found not a new client, or even an existing one.

Mitch.

He stood in taut silence, thumbs hooked in the back

pockets of his worn jeans. Juliette stared at his profile. An urge to touch him, feel his arms around her, assailed her with a pang so sharp, her stomach cramped.

With a sudden turn, he faced her. “I’ve been waiting for you to call me back. I was afraid something was wrong or you’d been hurt.”

She tried not to allow his concern to soften her. “Mr. MacKinnon, surely you understand the significance of an unreturned phone call.” She smiled tightly. “No comment.”

Mitch strode closer, jaw clenched, looking totally determined. “The article. I didn’t expect you to like it.”

“Since it’s pretty close to a personal attack, how could I? You barely stopped short of stating that I’m a total idiot and I have no right to be in business.”

He grabbed her shoulders. “I didn’t even hint at anything like that. You have every right to be in business. I think that, at least in our case, your system worked.”

She scoffed. And no, her hands were *not* trembling. “You didn’t state that for your readers, did you? To my recollection you only said that I’m inadequate in the screening of my clients.”

“Don’t do this,” he said, yanking her closer. “That article isn’t about us.”

“How can you say that?” She wriggled from his grasp. “You publicly humiliated me.”

“That wasn’t my intention, baby,” Mitch argued. “I swear. Besides, this was the last article. Nothing I wrote had anything to do with you and me and the future. It was a job.”

“How do you know they won’t ask you to write another? Louise Cannon tells me your articles about A Perfect Match have been the talk of the town. Apparently, circulation is up.

Why would they put a stop to something so successful?"

He stared down at the worn toes of his hiking boots. "You gotta trust me when I tell you there won't be any more articles."

"Trust you? Trust *you*!" She stared at him with her mouth gaping open. "After what you've written, I'm not sure I trust you as—"

"I promise you, not another printed word about your business."

"How can you promise me that?"

He looked away. "I just can."

She peered at him suspiciously. "What if John Cannon demands that you write another article?"

"He can't do that."

"Of course he can," she argued. "He's your boss, isn't he?"

Mitch swore. "Juliette, look. I..."

As he raked his fingers through his hair, her mind whirled. There was only way John Cannon couldn't force Mitch to write another article about her business: If Mitch no longer worked for John or *The Signal.*

Shock swirled in a heavy, mind-numbing flow throughout her. Vaguely, she was aware of the phone ringing in the background, of Mitch's agitated stance, of the smell of musk and wind that clung to him.

"You see, I got this phone call..." he continued.

The puzzle pieces fell into place, and she gasped. "You're moving, aren't you?"

His gaze sprang up to meet hers. Before he said a word, she saw the confirmation of her suspicion in his dark, troubled eyes. Her stomach plummeted to her knees. Tears stung the back of her eyes as she swung away.

“How did it happen?” Was that cracking, breathless thing her voice?

“Russ Kendrick, the editor-in-chief of *USA Today* called me on Christmas eve. He liked my series on your business, as well as my sports writing.” He stepped closer and brushed the back of his hand across her cheek. “For what it’s worth, I hated writing every word about you and A Perfect Match.”

As comprehension dawned, Juliette pulled away. The jerk! She’d tear him limb from limb, making sure she destroyed some limbs before others.

“You used me! You trashed my business, then used those works to climb your career ladder.”

“That was never intentional. I was only assigned this story because my coworker went into premature labor. I always, *always* intended to get Russ Kendrick’s attention via my sports writing.”

“God, who knows if even a word of that is true.”

He grasped her arm. “Juliette, baby—”

“Don’t ‘baby’ me.” She shook his grip away. “You lied to me about your article, you talked me out of marrying Andrew. Then, when I break it off with him and decide to explore what’s between us, what do you do? Tell me you’re off on your next big adventure.”

“Wait! You said ‘no’ to Andrew. You want to be with me? When did this happen?”

She ranted on, “And you, you care so much about me, you can’t even deliver your own damn Christmas gift, much less stay in the same town for more than six months.”

“You got the skates? How—”

“Never mind the skates!” She restrained an urge to stomp her foot. “It’s the fact you refuse to show up when you should or be a stable part of my life we're discussing."

"That's not true—"

"So you're not moving?" she challenged.

"Well, yes, but... I want you to come with me."

Come with me. Those three words were like a blow to the gut.

"Leave my sister, my business, my friends for a temporary town. Washington this week. Who knows, it may be India the next. I can't live like that."

"They don't have football in India," he pointed out.

"India or Indiana. It may as well be the same. It's another move."

Mitch narrowed his eyes with speculation. "Are you saying that if I move one inch out of Santa Clarita Valley, you won't have anything to do with me?"

She lifted her chin stubbornly. "I can't be with an ambition and adventure-seeker. I'm grateful that you helped me realize I shouldn't marry Andrew, but I can't just give up all semblance of security just so you can chase your next rainbow."

"So, it's either your way or no way?"

God, he made her sound so selfish, when self-preservation was all she sought.

"If that's how you want to look at it."

He shrugged. "I don't see any other view."

"So you're going?" She snapped her fingers. "Just like that, with no regrets? With no remorse for what might have been if you had been content to stay here?"

He frowned, his brows slashing down in pain. "I'm going with a lot of regrets. The biggest one being that I couldn't show you what a great life we could have had, that I couldn't prove that it doesn't matter where we are; what matters is that we're together."

"I won't follow you all over the planet like a lost puppy."

"And I can't stay here and continue grow professionally. If I can't take a shot at my dream, I'll be miserable."

Tears welled in the bottom of her eyes. Why did this hurt so badly? She'd always known this day would come.

But she never thought she'd love him until her heart wanted to shatter from the pain.

"You're choosing your career over your heart. We have nothing left to say," she whispered, and turned toward her office.

Every step down the hall, away from Mitch, felt like a mistake, which was nothing short of ridiculous. Mitch didn't understand that without security, she couldn't be happy. Which meant that he couldn't be trusted with her heart.

But if turning away from him wasn't a mistake, why did every muscle feel tighter than the spring on a mouse trap? Her foolish heart wanted to turn back and fling herself into his arms, and say she'd follow him anywhere.

"Don't turn your back on me."

She stopped halfway down the hallway. Fat tears rolled down her cheeks.

Mitch approached on silent footsteps. "This is likely a long-term move. Probably a decade at least. Come with me, just this once. Build a new life with me."

"And what about my business?"

"We'll rebuild it. Or, better yet, make it Internet-based. Please, Juliette. I've wanted this job my whole life. Can't you at least consider it?"

She inhaled raggedly, holding in a sob. "I already gave you

my heart. It obviously wasn't enough."

Juliette ran the rest of the way to her office.

"Wait!"

Mitch's voice rang in her ears as she slammed the door to her office. Hearing the entreaty in his voice only would only make her wonder more if she could move with Mitch. Knowing that uprooting her life was against everything she wanted and had worked for, that her hope he cared enough to stay was futile, only multiplied her pain.

Moments later, he knocked on the door. Juliette closed her eyes, as if blocking her view of the door would make her less apt to open it.

"Juliette, baby. Open the door, please."

A tempting thought, but no. She had to be true to herself. She wanted security. She'd made Santa Clarita her home and had no desire to follow another man all over the country for his career. No doubt about it, spending even another evening with Mitch, much less contemplating a lifetime with him, could only lead to a shattered heart.

"Listen, please..." Mitch said through the closed door. "I love you."

Her heart burst into a thousand tiny pieces. Why did he have to confess his feelings now, when it was too late?

After a full minute of silence, Mitch finally said, "I'm sorry. I didn't mean to hurt you."

Underneath the door, he slid a business card. Juliette stared at the white square for a few hard seconds before curiosity overcame her.

She pushed away from her desk chair and retrieved the ivory scrap of paper. On the front lay Mitch's name, the title "Sports Journalist," and *The Signal*'s logo.

"On the back," he said, his voice penetrating her office door, "is my new office phone number. You have my cell number. Like I said, I'll call you when I get settled."

She sighed and pressed the card between her fingers until they turned white.

"You're a special woman, Juliette. I mean that." He paused. "If...if you change your mind about giving us a chance, call me."

Retreating footsteps signaled Mitch's departure, possibly from her life. She should be happy. No more dilemmas. She could start over and create her own life. She didn't need a man to be happy. Her business and her family would be her mainstays.

But she felt as if every cell inside her were collapsing into the black hole of her heart. That she would never be whole again.

Chapter Ten

Juliette's next two weeks passed quietly, punctuated by unseasonably cold weather and her melancholy tears. She allowed Kara to drag her to a New Year's Eve party littered with wonderfully happy couples eager to kiss at the stroke of midnight. Her own sister had met a new guy and indulged in the "Auld Lang Syne" tradition. Juliette stood in the corner, sipping champagne punch and wondering what the adventuresome Mitch was doing and who he might be kissing. Her vow not to cry again lasted only as long as her drive home.

He hadn't called since that disastrous day at her office. She had rushed home the night they'd parted, half hoping he had called to say that his most recent move didn't rank as more important than the life they might have together. No such luck. He was clearly waiting for her to "compromise".

Trouble was, she missed Mitch—terribly. Maybe she should give in. But she wondered about the next time he wanted to pursue a new career path, which would inevitably require another move. What then? Would he be willing to compromise and stay put?

The first week of January became the second. Business had picked up some. Thank God for New Year's resolutions. She had even given the police some clues that aided in finding Rexelle Kramer, which helped to settle Joe Tarton's rancor.

At a local Mexican food restaurant two nights ago, she had bumped into Andrew. He'd been civil, thank goodness. Maybe someday, they'd be friends again. He'd introduced her to his date. They actually looked perfect together. Life was working out wonderfully...

For everyone but her.

With a sigh, she rose from her desk and wandered toward the coffee maker. She checked all the cabinets before remembering she hadn't bought coffee recently. Ingesting extra caffeine when she already couldn't sleep through the night probably wasn't a good idea. Maybe some juice would be better.

She grabbed her wallet and walked next door to The Brunchery. Inside the little restaurant, she bought a bagel and spotted a can of pineapple-mango juice in the refrigerated case, which just reminded her of Mitch.

With a sorrowful smile, she reflected on their magical first date. She passed the can of juice by and opted for hot apple cider, instead.

And she couldn't resist the latest copy of *The Signal.*

Juliette had purchased several editions of the paper in the last week, but hadn't seen a single printed word from Mitch. She wanted him to be happy, wanted him to enjoy his job.

But she wanted him to be happy with her, here in Santa Clarita.

She took a leisurely stroll back to her office, then spread out her breakfast and newspaper. She had an appointment after lunch, but between now and then, she had only to contend with bothersome paperwork she'd been avoiding for weeks.

She skimmed the front page before flipping to the next. An article on page two caught her eye immediately.

A Real Life Perfect Match by Mitchell E. MacKinnon

Mitch? Hope rose, followed by her curiosity. Was he back in Santa Clarita and writing for *The Signal* again?

Dating services are for drips; their owners are nothing but scam artists...at least that was my impression before meeting Juliette Lowell, the owner of local dating service A Perfect Match. How quickly she proved me wrong.

During one of our first interviews, Ms. Lowell challenged me to become a believer by inviting me to register as one of her clients. When I accepted, she also bet me that I'd meet my future wife on my prearranged date. After I finished laughing, I told her if that ever happened, I would write her the biggest endorsement The Santa Clarita Signal *has ever seen.*

After getting to know the lovely Ms. Lowell, who happened to be my perfect match, according to her matchmaking system, I'm here to eat crow and pay up. I don't know if her secret is her intuition, her computer program, or heck, it might even be her astrological profiles, but whatever the trick, her system, in my case, was honestly, truly effective. If she can find the perfect woman for a doubter like me, she can work wonders for anyone ready for a new relationship.

Juliette gasped. Her eyes watered. Did he really mean that?

So now that I've lived up to my part of the bargain and given A Perfect Match my most glowing endorsement, I'm wondering if Ms. Lowell will live up to her end and do me the honor of becoming my wife?

Juliette's numb fingers released the paper. She barely saw it drift to the floor.

His wife? She trembled, fought off a wave of dizzy pleasure and fear. How did he think they would work their differences out? Or did he expect her to give in and move?

Her heart pounded in a *thump-thump* rhythm. She had to have the answers to her questions—now.

Digging out his business card with trembling hands, she tried his cell phone. Voicemail. Damn, now what... *The Signal*! Maybe John Cannon would know where he was.

A quick phone call later, and Juliette knew that Mitch was back in the area, but not in *The Signal's* offices at the moment.

Where could that wonderful, confounding man be?

Racing to the bathroom, she applied fresh lipstick, so she would look decent when she found him. On her way out, she grabbed her purse.

Before she could make a clean getaway, the electronic chime sounded, signaling someone had come through her door. She groaned. Great, she needed to hunt down the man of her dreams, and instead, she was probably going to be waylaid by a client.

She ran down the hall with a ready "can I help you?" on her tongue. In the entryway stood Mitch, his face tense with uncertainty. In one hand, he sported a bouquet of flowers, in the other, a copy of *The Signal*.

"Hi," he greeted quietly. "I was hoping you might have a few minutes to talk."

She stepped closer, eyeing the massive collection of roses, carnations, daisies, irises and lilies he carried with awe.

"Those are gorgeous," she said.

"So are you."

She took the flowers from him before sending him a questioning stare. "You deliver your own flowers but not your Christmas gifts?"

He flashed her a self-deprecating grin, complete with dimples, and dropped his gaze to the ground. "That was when I had a shocking job offer and thought you needed space...and I wondered if pursuing you would be as practical as giving myself a lobotomy."

"And now?" she queried, her heart lifting.

"I rented a great apartment near D.C. and met terrific neighbors. I have amazing co-workers and found a perfect little Thai restaurant just around the corner from my new office."

Juliette swallowed a lump of disappointment. So he was here to sell her on the greatness of the other side of the country.

She sighed. Everyone seemed to be getting on with life but her. Mitch was happier away from Santa Clarita. And eventually, when she stopped loving him she'd be happier, too. Or maybe...one move wouldn't be so terrible? Because she had a feeling she wouldn't get over the man until sometime in the ninety-ninth century.

"I'm really happy for you," she forced herself to say.

"I'm miserable without you," he groaned and reached for her hands. "God, I've missed you. I tried living without you. And I don't want to do it anymore. I tried to make you see that security didn't mean anything if you weren't with people you love. I still think that's the case, but I realize that the same was true about a new town or a better job. It was hard to care when I hurt so badly. Losing you just slammed home the fact that life is about who you share it with. The rest...is distraction and window dressing. But none of it gives you the kind of meaning that loving someone does."

What did that mean for them? They loved each other, and

she no longer wanted to be without him. If he needed to be in D.C., that's where she'd go.

Juliette felt tears needle the back of her eyes. "Really?"

He didn't respond to her question. He simply handed her the newspaper. "I brought you a copy of today's *Signal.*"

She smiled. Hope burst like a spectacle of fireworks within her. "I have a copy in my office."

He tried to appear nonchalant. The tense set of his jaw and shoulders gave him away. "Read page two yet?"

"About ten minutes ago."

Suddenly, he yanked on her hand and drew her closer. "Before you say a word, I know you're worried about moving. I've thought all that through," he assured. "I was doing okay at *The Signal.* If moving means the difference between yes and no, I'll quit *USA Today* and get my old job back. We'll stay here in Santa Clarita. I want you to be happy being with me. I'll be happy being with you, no matter where we are."

Tears sprang to her eyes and fell to her cheeks. Unmitigated joy swelled and churned within her like a river during a flood.

He was willing to sacrifice his ambition and wanderlust for her. He was prepared to indulge her need for security and community at his own expense.

As Mitch brushed her tears away, she realized he deserved the same.

Sniffling with joy, she set the flowers aside and walked into his embrace. "You don't have to do that for me."

His frown displayed genuine confusion. "You said that to be happy, you needed to be here with your family and your business..."

"I was wrong."

He held her tightly. “You don’t have to move. I’ll stay here, if that’s what you need.”

She shook her head. “You know, I figured something out, too. I guess I’ve known it in my head for awhile. The realization just took some time to reach my heart.”

Mitch stood, watching her. His thumb stroked the back of her hand. “What’s that?”

“That four walls don’t make a secure home. Love does. Only when people want to be together and support each other can you have real security,” she explained. “I mean, neighbors and friends are nice to have, and continuity will always be important to me.” She reached out, stroked his cheek. “But not more important than you. I’ll be happy being with you, too, no matter where we are.”

He held her face, his gaze probing deep into her eyes. “Is that a yes?”

The smile that spread across her face seemed to come from deep within, starting and finishing in a never-ending circle at her heart. “Yes.”

He let loose a holler of triumph and held her closer. “Baby, I swear we’ll work it out. I’ll come back to *The Signal*, and in another year or two, another opportunity closer to Santa Clarita will present itself. Maybe with the *L.A. Times*. And we can still live right here.”

“I think I’ve got another plan, a compromise,” she clarified. “Kara hates her job, and I’d have no trouble persuading her to run this office, I’ll bet. I could open another one in D.C. Business would be hard at first, but I think—”

“Baby? Let’s work out the details later,” he said, then lowered his mouth to hers. “First, I’ve got to kiss you.”

One kiss, sweet and slow, led to another. Mitch held her tight, caressing his way up her arms to anchor his hands in her hair, around her nape. He drew her closer and moved in again, deeper. Juliette moaned as the kiss heated.

The man flat knew how to kiss, as if it was an end all its own, not a prelude to anything else. Like he had all day long to taste her mouth. So sexy and thorough...

Juliette inched closer and curled one of her legs around his, her hands around his neck.

He broke the kiss to whisper, "Cuddling up to me like that is going to get you in trouble."

"What kind of trouble?" She sent him a saucy smile.

Then he pressed against her, proving he was more than ready to dish out trouble.

"Got an hour?"

"For you, I have a lifetime."

"If I'm very good, will you start proving it to me now?"

"I could be...persuaded."

Before she could take another breath, Mitch picked her up, urged her legs around his hips—which lifted her skirt up shorter than the most micro-mini—and carried her down the hall.

"What... Where are you going?"

A few moments later, he stormed into her office and kicked the door shut behind him. "I'm getting you all alone so I can persuade you...at length."

She giggled—until he reached under her skirt and pulled her panties down. "Here? Seriously?"

"Very seriously."

Then he covered her mouth with his own. The kiss passed hot and soared into blistering territory. Never, in all the times they'd kissed, had he tasted more determined. The woman in her liked his aggressive side, and sighed when her panties hit the floor. Then started counting the seconds until he did something similar with her bra.

"You're a very bad influence on me. You're turning me into a sex fiend."

"God, I hope so," he groaned with one hand making short work of her blouse, and the other inching under her skirt and over her thighs.

Mitch's touch started that head-to-toe tingle only he could give her.

In moments, her snowy blouse hit some distant corner of her desk, her bra found a far-flung corner, and Mitch discovered an oral fixation for her nipples. She gripped his short hair in her fist and enjoyed his obsession.

Long moments later, he paused for a breath—and to rip his shirt off. Then he kneeled, pushed her skirt up and continued to demonstrate the fact he was both orally fascinated and gifted.

Red-hot cheeks and two orgasms later, she was panting and more than happy to lie back on her desk and let him do his wickedest.

As he paused to protect them and sank deep, she gasped and gladly took him inside her.

"Oh, God. You fit me perfectly. The pleasure is going to kill me." His voice shook.

"It better not. You owe me lots of years."

"I can't believe I'm lucky enough to share them with you. You have one hell of a matchmaking system, soon-to-be Mrs. MacKinnon."

"Told you so." Then she gasped when he sank deep again, the friction driving her mad.

"Thank God you did." He kissed her reverently, passionately, a melding of mouths, breaths and hearts. "I love you."

"I love you, too. Now what were you doing before we started talking?"

Mitch smiled. "Oh, this?"

He plunged deep, gripping her as if nothing else was important to him—or ever would be.

"Yes. Exactly that. Don't stop."

And he didn't stop until her cries filled up the room.

ଔ

Four days later, Juliette heard the click of Mitch opening the door of his truck. She wiggled her nose, silently protesting the blindfold he'd placed over her eyes.

"Okay," he said. "Step down."

She groped for his hand. "Where the heck are you leading me?"

He sighed as he helped her out of his truck. "For the tenth time this hour, it's a surprise."

Cool air whispered against her legs. Her dress brushed her calves.

She inhaled a deep breath. "I smell salt."

In the distance, the sound of waves churning against the shoreline seeped into her senses. "What are we doing at the beach? Is this why you insisted I wear my new skates with this dress?"

He shut the truck's door. "It's a surprise, already. Just give me two more minutes, okay?" He helped her glide forward.

"God, you're more impatient than mom's dog at chow time."

"I'm not impatient, I'm curious," she corrected.

"Same difference."

They rolled forward on the pavement. Juliette was dying to pull at the blindfold Mitch insisted she wear and find out what he had planned. After all, inline skating by the beach in semi-formal attire was pretty strange.

He coached her to a slow stop finally, then whispered. "I brought you here today because this is where I first thought I might be in love with you." He kissed her lips. "I was right."

Juliette's heart swelled. "I love you, too."

"Good. Are you ready?"

She smiled, nearly bouncing with anticipation. "Yes."

"Really ready?"

"Get on with it!"

He laughed and thrust something soft, sweet-smelling and stick-like into her hand. Reflexively, she grabbed it as Mitch pulled away her blindfold.

Juliette blinked. Was that a minister standing beneath a white arch? And flowers all around. People, all in after-five dress, stood on either side of the arch, silhouetted against the sunset. And the item Mitch had put into her hands was a bouquet of flowers and ribbons. This looked like a—

Her mouth opened wide with shock. "Is this a surprise wedding?"

"Yeah. I wanted to do something really wild to show you what you mean to me. I figured if other people can skydive while exchanging vows, a surprise on skates wouldn't be so odd. What do you say?"

Juliette looked over the crowd. Kara and her beau stood toward the front, holding hands. Her father, dressed in a crisp, dark suit, smiled at her. On the right side of the arch, Mitch's mother stood. Beside Gianna, Juliette spotted Louise Cannon, whom she knew from the beauty shop, and a man she assumed to be Louise's husband, John.

This was perfect, so different from the black-tie event Andrew had wanted. This wedding would be a symbolic expression of the love she and Mitch shared—traditional and romantic, with a little twist.

Juliette felt tears at the back of her eyes. "I don't know what to say."

"Say yes. We'll be really different," he cajoled.

"It's awfully romantic."

"What do you say?" His voice was hopeful.

She reached for his hand. "Absolutely yes. I couldn't have planned it better myself."

Mitch laughed.

"No wonder you insisted we get our marriage licenses as soon as I said yes." Then she gasped. "I don't have your ring yet."

"Your sister and I took care of finding yours and mine yesterday."

"You thought of everything," she said, certain she was glowing pink with happiness.

"I gave it my best shot. I wasn't going to wait another ten minutes, just in case you changed your mind. I want you to be all mine now."

Mitch gestured to her father, who came forward to take Juliette's arm. Kara produced a portable CD player as Mitch took his place at the makeshift altar. At the touch of a button, the "Wedding March" filled the air, in conjunction with the gentle lapping of the ocean against the sand.

"You look happy," her father said, leading her toward Mitch, toward her future. "I think you made the right choice."

She smiled, tears filling her eyes. "Me, too."

Ten minutes later, Mitch kissed her thoroughly amidst the clapping crowd, and she was Juliette MacKinnon—a very happy woman. She glanced at the row of brilliant diamonds spanning her wedding band, then smiled at her husband.

After the ceremony, they mingled among the small gathering of family and friends, hands clasped. Mitch's mother cried and welcomed her to the family with a hug. Her father shook Mitch's hand and drew him into a discussion about the upcoming Super Bowl.

They cut a small multi-tiered cake resting on a decorated table on the far side of the arch and sipped at a little punch. Married. She still couldn't believe it!

Then Juliette tossed her bouquet. To everyone's delight, Kara caught it.

"Let's get out of here," Mitch murmured moments later. "I've smiled until my face is stiff. Unfortunately, so is something else, and my mind is wandering."

Juliette giggled. "You're terrible."

"Because you make me crazy. I love you."

"I love you, too," she said and kissed him as they waved goodbye to the crowd.

As they headed to the truck, he mentioned, "I got a phone call yesterday from a guy at the *L.A. Times*, wanting to know if I want a job. There, or back to D. C. Your call..."

She smiled and squeezed his hand. "No, whatever we decide, we'll do it together. We'll compromise."

He dragged her closer, wearing a devilish grin. "I'll compromise you anytime, baby. It'll be my pleasure."

About the Author

To learn more about Shelley Bradley please visit her website, www.shelleybradley.com. Send an email to Shelley at shelley@shelleybradley.com, friend her on MySpace at www.myspace.com/shelleybradley or join her Yahoo! group to participate in the fun with other readers and Wicked Writers, as well as Shelley!

http://groups.yahoo.com/group/wicked_writers.

A woman craves. A man wants.
Their collision pitches them into the hot zone.

Private Maneuvers

© 2008 Denise A. Agnew

Hot Zone

Sometimes a woman craves what she shouldn't want...

Marisa Clyde wants nothing to do with the soldier acting as a temporary bouncer in her uncle's tavern, even though the stoic, six-feet-of-smoldering hunk rescued her during a tour gone bad in Mexico. While those few short moments sent their sexual tension screaming off the charts, a devastating hurt in her past now blocks her willingness to surrender to him. He'll only be in town a month. If she can just wait it out, he'll soon be out of her life.

Sometimes a man wants more than a woman is willing to share...

Jake Sullivan watches Marisa like a hawk, well aware his need to protect is messing with his mind and making him care way more than he should. Priding himself on clinical detachment in the game between man and woman, he figures once he's slept with her, she'll be out of his system for good. But that's before he experiences her at a deeper level—and learns she just might be in danger again.

Enjoy the following excerpt from Private Maneuvers...

The second Marisa Clyde saw the soldier she knew he was trouble.

He took Marisa's hand as she stepped off the old tour bus. Huge fingers and a big palm wrapped her much smaller hand. Her body shivered as warmth flickered in her stomach. In fact, her entire body quaked.

He looked like rescue.

He looked like safety wrapped up in one sexy, strong, powerful package.

She could blame it on the events of the last twenty-four hours. Danger and fear could rattle a person. Or just perhaps, it could be this man and the power he emanated.

Maybe the long, thick lashes framing the onyx eyes staring down into hers influenced her senses to scatter. She was nuts to go completely ga-ga over the man standing in front of her when she *refused* to find a military man attractive ever again. Maybe she could blame her reaction to him on the heat wavering upward from the washboard surface of the road and the relentless sun beating down. Or perhaps the humidity level coming from the Mexican jungle all around them had steamed her brains. Of course, the fact that her ribs had taken a bit of beating didn't help. Every time she breathed, a dull ache radiated outward from her left side.

Not what she expected to experience on a vacation, but she'd made it through worse and lived to tell about it.

As her Uncle Dexter back in Clarksville, Wyoming would say, the pucker factor for the last day had escalated way off the charts. She had a right to feel disoriented, hungry, and exhausted. A smear on her glasses irritated her, but she didn't bother to try and clean it. Face it, a smear was so not that important when she'd just survived what would amount in the news to an international incident.

Her ribs panged, and she winced.

"Are you all right, ma'am?" the soldier asked, his deep voice a husky sound that brushed along her senses like a feather tickling all her erogenous zones.

She couldn't answer him. Through her tiredness, her hormones registered that he stood around six three or four, his muscular build apparent through the camo wear. He wore no rank or insignia that could identify him.

His military short obsidian hair gleamed with blue highlights under the fierce sun. He topped the charts into unbelievably gorgeous. *No. Not exactly.* Dark and dangerous, a huge cliché, didn't explain the unique mix-and-match hardness in his features that added up to one handsome visage. Yet dangerous certainly described his aura, a kick-butt-and-don't-bother-to-take-names presence. His angular face defied description—his jaw formed a solid frame around his hard mouth. His nose was a smidgen crooked. Those intriguing, mysterious eyes didn't hide anything. Did he know how his feelings gleamed so starkly in his gaze? Probably not. Right now his eyes narrowed, as if he wanted to read her mind and excavate answers.

When she didn't answer him, his gaze turned dark, serious and concerned. "Ma'am?"

"Poor dear is a bit shocky," Ida Hambly said behind her. "She's had quite an ordeal."

"I'm fine," Marisa said. "There's nothing wrong with me."

"Right. Nothing wrong. You've just made it through a bombing, a robbery, and a broken down bus. All in a day's work for an accountant?" Ida leaned heavily on her cane, and when the soldier saw Ida hesitating on the bottom step of the bus, he released Marisa's hand and helped the elderly woman down and over to where Marisa stood. "And then the cavalry rides in on white horses and saves our butts. I'd say that's enough to rattle your sweet young cage."

Marisa smirked. "Ida, your sense of humor kept me sane."

That, and maybe Freddie Bodine. Freddie stood clasped in the arms of her boyfriend, another one of the soldiers who'd come to the rescue. Apparently he'd traveled from the U.S. after putting together this team of army men to look for Freddie when the tour bus went missing and didn't report back to the hotel.

Freddie's head pressed against her boyfriend's shoulder, and his hand cupped the back of her head. He touched his lips to the top of Freddie's head in a tender gesture. He looked drained with relief. *What would it feel like to have a man love me that much?*

Ten other soldiers who'd first appeared earlier like ghosts from the jungle entered the bus. People chattered in excited, relieved voices and the soldiers hurried to extract them from the vehicle.

Trauma of the last day worked into her sore body. The back of her neck ached, muscles in her lower back protested. She stretched and arched her back, as she sighed. She felt grungy, her long hair frizzing in the humidity, her khaki shorts and plain blue T-shirt rumpled. She regretted the movement as pain arched through her side again.

Damn it.

"You should have seen how Marisa and Freddie convinced those bastards to take nothing else but the cash," Ida said to one of the soldiers. "It was truly amazing."

Marisa's legs started to tremble, and her temples throbbed.

As if he had radar for her emotional or physical changes, her soldier's gaze flicked her way and he frowned as he eyeballed her. He spoke into a satellite phone and ordered another person to bring their transportation. She rubbed the back of her neck and allowed her eyes to slip closed.

The soldier's voice rumbled nearby, and she opened her eyes to find him within her personal space. So close she should have rebelled. She never let men get this close—until now. He gripped Marisa's upper arm as if he expected her to collapse any minute. She'd never felt this fragile before, hanging by a single thread combined of liberation and leftover fear.

"Ma'am—Marisa, would you like some water?" He handed her a small water bottle.

It took her a few seconds to respond. She irrationally wanted to tell him to call her Miss Clyde or ma'am because she wanted the distance and formality.

Instead she said, "Thank you."

She took the water and slammed back a huge swallow. She knew better than to gulp the lukewarm liquid, but thirst compelled her to slug down half the bottle. Immediately her stomach lurched in protest.

"Whoa. Slow down," he said.

She glared at him. "I'm thirsty."

"Drink too much and it'll make you sick."

"I know."

She almost stalked away. Not because she found him repulsive. Nope. She found him way, way too intriguing.

She heard the rumble of vehicles and two large vans turned the corner and progressed their way. Tension shot up her back.

"There's our transport," her soldier said.

Good. Lethargy weighed her down, as if she sank into her

athletic shoes a few inches, quicksand sucking her into blessed darkness.

His voice sounded too far away, and then as her head seemed to float and her legs turned rubbery, she managed to whisper a plea, "Wait..."

He moved toward her quickly. "What's wrong?"

"I—I don't think I can—"

Her eyelids fluttered and suddenly his powerful arms encircled her. "Easy. Are you hurt somewhere and just not telling us about it?"

Marisa clutched at his shoulders. "My ribs. One of the bandits slung me into a seat." She touched her glasses, held together in the middle by some tape Ida had found in her voluminous tote bag. "That's how I broke my glasses."

"Son of a bitch." Her soldier growled the words under his breath.

He lifted her in his arms, and she said, "No. I mean, I'm fine. It's not that big a deal."

He carried her toward the vans. "Sergeant Clearwater! We need a medic."

Freddie, Ida, and Freddie's soldier followed, Freddie's and Ida's concerned voices echoing in her ears.